A gift ?

Neil D.

Under a

Mallorcan Sky

Neil Doloughan

Grosvenor House
Publishing Limited

All rights reserved
Copyright © Neil Doloughan, 2014

The right of Neil Doloughan to be identified as the author of this
work has been asserted by him in accordance with Section 78
of the Copyright, Designs and Patents Act 1988

The book cover picture is copyright to Neil Doloughan

This book is published by
Grosvenor House Publishing Ltd
28-30 High Street, Guildford, Surrey, GU1 3EL.
www.grosvenorhousepublishing.co.uk

This book is sold subject to the conditions that it shall not, by way of
trade or otherwise, be lent, resold, hired out or otherwise circulated
without the author's or publisher's prior consent in any form of binding or
cover other than that in which it is published and
without a similar condition including this condition being imposed
on the subsequent purchaser.

This book is a work of fiction. Most of the locations named exist, but the
situations and scenes described are imaginary and although some of the
characters are based on real people their names have been changed.
In relation to those characters not based on real people any similarity
to any person living or dead is purely coincidental.

A CIP record for this book
is available from the British Library

ISBN 978-1-78148-715-0

This book is dedicated to Police officers throughout the world who provide a necessary service to us all, often in dangerous circumstances. In particular, those who have been killed or injured as a result of terrorist actions whilst performing their duty, such as Carlos Saenz de Tejada Garcia and Diego Salva Lezaun, two Guardia Civil officers killed by an ETA car bomb in Palma Nova, Mallorca on 30th July, 2009. I was 2 miles away on that day and heard the explosion. There but for the grace of God, go I.

"You cannot have good without evil,
nor beauty without ugliness,
nor compassion without cruelty,
for how can you appreciate one without the other?"

Neil Doloughan, Under a Mallorcan Sky

Contents

1

A STRANGE FISH

The clock on the church of San Bartolomeu, which looked down on the miniscule but picturesque plaça in the centre of Fornalutx struck ten. James appeared at the top of the steps, ready to descend the flight to the bottom, like a debutante, in full view of the many locals and tourists that filled the tables outside Café sa Plaça and Bar Deportivo. The sun had all but disappeared behind the Sierra de Tramuntana Mountains, which surround the village. The last of its rays reflected a pink hue against the rock visible between the pine and olive trees, framed by the French-inspired architecture of the golden stone and green-shuttered houses that made Fornalutx such a treat for the eyes. By the time he had reached the bottom, the clock chimed ten for a second time. It was a Mallorcan superstitious quirk meant to fool 'el diablo' or more probably for the benefit of the workers in the fields. The air was thick with a blend of many conversations in numerous languages, the clinking of glasses and plates, interspersed with the shrill, excited shrieks of young children as they chased one another across the

1

square and up the steps, wooden swords in hand. It was just a typical August evening.

James scanned the tables and their occupants, squinting like a drill sergeant might inspect regimented rows on a parade ground, in an effort to find a recognisable face through a sea of invaders of the holidaying-kind, which was no mean task for a man with an aversion to wearing his prescription glasses. To his right, James recognised the unmistakeable figures of his elderly Mallorcan neighbour, Marta coming towards him, arm in arm with Magdelena, her daughter.

"Buenas tardes," came the greeting in unison, "Que tal?"

"Muy bien," replied James, which was almost his full repertoire of Spanish.

"Donde esta el simpatico?" Marta asked, enquiring as to the whereabouts of James' son Adam.

"En la casa," replied James, gesturing up the steps with his hand.

Most conversations with Marta consisted of a mix of Castilian Spanish and Catalan from her and English peppered with basic Spanish and lots of hand gesturing from him. Taking lessons in both Spanish and Catalan was a priority for James and he was to start the following week but for now international sign language would have to do.

He found respite in the form of his friends Matt and Jayne and after bidding goodnight to his neighbours, he joined his friends at their table.

"What will it be? Beer? Mojito?" asked Matt.

"Em... I think I'll have a mojito," replied James, before kissing Jayne in greeting and taking a seat at the table.

James had known Matt and Jayne for a few years and felt at ease in their company. He admired their 'joie de vivre' and their courage in moving permanently to Mallorca with a young family, taking on a new business in order to achieve a more family-orientated, outdoor lifestyle. This was a big departure from being a BBC reporter in Belfast during 'The Troubles' for Matt. Indeed, on their first meeting in Mallorca, both James and Matt realised they had met before at various gruesome murder scenes in Northern Ireland, when James had been a detective there. Nothing could be further from James' mind as he breathed in the heady, intoxicating aromas of a Mallorcan summer evening, coupled with the feeling that this little place really was paradise on earth and with the expectant satisfaction of Pepe's fresh mint mojito, life couldn't have been better.

"What have you been up to today?" asked James.

"I tried to finish some work on the kitchen but it was too nice a day to be inside, so we went for a swim at Repic and then I took Jamie fishing at the harbour end of the Port," replied Matt.

Just then the familiar shape of a gaunt, giant of a man produced a mojito from a metal tray and placed it in front of James. It was Pepe the amiable Swedish barman.

"A Pepe Special for you James. How are the boys? I haven't seen them today," he said.

"Yeah, they're good. They were at the beach today and they are feeling tired for a change," replied James.

One of the deciding factors which made James bring his family to live in Mallorca and in particular Fornalutx, apart from the Mediterranean climate and stunning scenery, was the cosmopolitan mix of people. James felt that it was true that Mallorca had its fair share of foreign residents from Germany and 'Blighty' but in James' village there were people from four continents who had decided to make it their home. Never mind 'the world's a global village', Fornalutx most certainly was.

What he liked most of all was the way Mallorcans both loved children and respected their elderly. Children were welcomed everywhere and grown men would demonstrably show fondness for babies and young children, whilst their respect for their elderly was no more evident than in Fornalutx itself when every year during the village fiesta in September, the whole village would turn out to celebrate and honour those residents over seventy years of age with a ceremony in the plaça. Local children would present a gift to each revered resident in turn as their name and age was read out by the Mayor.

The conversation continued as Pepe returned to his duties and the evening wore on seamlessly. James, on returning to the table from the toilet, found a dark, heavy-set man, in his late thirties, sitting with Matt and Jayne. James took his seat, whilst observing the stranger who was in conversation with Matt and whose gaze was only broken by Matt's arm gesturing towards James.

"Steve, isn't it?" asked Matt.

The man nodded in acknowledgement.

"This is James." A relaxed hand was pushed in James' direction.

"Alright mate. Pleased to meet you," came the greeting in a distinct London accent.

James' hand was extended across the table. "Likewise," he said.

4

A round of drinks arrived at the table courtesy of the new arrival.

Matt continued, "Steve here has recently bought a house just past Café Med."

"Oh right. Why Fornalutx?" asked James, taking a sip of his drink.

"Well you know, it's lovely and people don't bother you here," came Steve's reply.

The conversation continued and all four enjoyed further drinks, until Jayne retired to bed and Matt made his half-hourly sortie to the gents, leaving James with his new acquaintance.

"What part of London are you from?" he asked.

"South London," came the reply.

"Where in south London?" persisted James.

"Bermondsey," said Steve bluntly.

"Oh right, whereabouts? I used to work there and I lived in Blackheath," said James.

"You're joking! Where'd you work?" asked the broody but now animated Steve, drawing the last drag on his cigarette before casually tossing it on the ground, an uneasy grin unable to hide the absence of two teeth either side of his incisors.

"Well," started James, "do you know Lower Road, just up from The Prince of Orange pub?"

"Yeah." Steve's mind appeared to be whirling and his smile quickly faded. "Are you 'Old Bill'?" asked Steve in a direct manner.

"Was," said James.

"When was you there?" asked Steve nonchalantly.

James felt as if Steve was merely trying to hide his evident displeasure at the realisation that he had travelled hundreds of miles only to discover that he was talking to an ex-cop from his old 'manor'. If alarm bells had not already been ringing in James' head, they were now.

James, through a necessary sense of self-preservation during his time in the Metropolitan Police and in particular The Royal Ulster Constabulary, had always had to size people up very quickly and tended to make assumptions based on his gut reaction. In the first few minutes of meeting Steve, he felt uneasy about this misfit. There was something not quite right about him. This fish out of water intrigued him. Steve's appearance was a juxtaposition between designer chic and 'chav'. A Tag Heuer watch and Ralph Lauren shirt were awkwardly accompanied by chunky gold necklaces and a gold sovereign ring. His overall appearance was rather unkempt and was indicative of a certain life-style, as was the missing teeth and a double scar on his left cheek. James had met many similar men over the years and it was frequently from the other side of a table, but usually it was in the presence of a solicitor with a tape running. This man may as well have had the word 'CRIMINAL' tattooed across his furrowed brow. But that was not what he found disturbing but fascinating at the same time. The question was: why this village? He could quite easily see Steve in any of the 'Brits abroad' type pubs in Magaluf but what had made him chose this village in which to live? He was intent on discovering the truth without alienating Steve and anyway, he could be wrong about him but he knew his gut was usually right.

"I was in Bermondsey in the early 1990's," said James.

"Right," said Steve. The answer appeared to lift his spirits as he lit another cigarette. "Fancy another?" he asked.

"Let me get these," said James. "Same again?"

"Sweet!" replied Steve.

Just then Matt returned as James motioned to Pepe to bring more drinks.

"There's nothing worse than people scrounging fags and I've supposed to have given up," started James towards Steve, "but would you mind?"

"Yeah, yeah. I didn't know you smoked mate," said Steve.

"Nor does my wife. I still like the odd one now and then," added James.

Steve pushed his packet of cigarettes and lighter towards James just as his mobile phone rang. He stood up to answer it and he walked slowly away from the table to the water fountain in the plaça a few yards away but out of ear shot. James carefully took out a cigarette from the packet and examined it, as if he had just been handed a priceless vase and lit it, drawing on it and exhaling smoke upwards in a deliberate, exaggerated way.

Turning to Matt he said, "I can't quite work him out."

Matt gave an agreeing nod.

"I've met him before in Soller, a couple of weeks ago. Brad introduced me to him. He's a bit of a wide boy but he's pleasant enough," said Matt.

From across the plaça James could hear Steve's voice get louder and he was now pacing up and down. Suddenly he returned to the table, his face drawn.

"I've got to nip home. I'll be back to finish my beer," said Steve.

"Everything alright?" enquired James.

"Yeah, yeah. See you in ten minutes."

With that, Steve turned and walked across the square in the direction of his street. Ten minutes soon became an hour and as the clock sounded one o'clock Matt turned to James and said,

"Right! I'd better make a move. Jamie's got a football match tomorrow in Palma and I've to drive him and a couple of his mates there. I don't think Steve is coming back tonight. I'll settle my bill with Pepe. Oh by the way are you working on the house tomorrow?"

"I am in the morning but we'll probably see you at the Port in the afternoon. Goodnight."

As Matt made his way home, James sat alone at his table in the plaça, with the last few remaining tourists. All the locals were by now in their beds. He liked this time of night. It was relatively peaceful and the old antique lanterns, long since bereft of their original oil, now shone on the cobbled streets and the church façade, which overlooked the plaça. The fronds of a nearby palm tree cast a spider-like shadow onto the high stone walls. He loved the narrow streets lined on either side by the tall townhouses tightly packed, in a deliberate way, designed by The Moors to protect against invaders and the elements.

The whole village was a maze of these narrow cobbled streets, just wide enough for a donkey and cart to pass, which was pretty much how it was up until the 1960's. It was only then that a proper road had been built to allow for modern cars to access into the heart of this one thousand year old village. The now mainly pedestrianised streets were lined with bougainvillea, ivy, ferns and an abundance of flowering plants in terracotta pots, adding to the splendour of this picture postcard oasis. Many of the historical aspects of the architecture of the village were still visible. There were still original painted and decorative roof tiles on some houses, as well as the village water fountains and the original communal village wash house with its spring mountain water, where some of the villages elderly women still washed their clothes in preference to modern washing machines. There was the castellated roof tower of the Council offices and the little walled graveyard on the edge of the village, towards a hamlet called Binabassi. Many of the houses retained their original antique wooden front doors, some of which would not have looked out of place on a medieval castle and the majority of houses had decorative tiles showing the house name invariably prefixed by the Catalan word 'Ca'n', meaning house of, followed by the surname of the local family who once lived there.

On the corner of the plaça James observed a four storey house, about one room wide, which he had been told was once where those responsible for minor misdemeanours would have been kept in its cells but now, like many other houses in the village over the last century, it had had some grander features added to what originally would have been a rustic rural house. A few had acquired ornate metalwork, such as wrought-iron balconies or window grilles and some had carved sandstone quoins, making the diversity of the architecture very appealing, whilst all blending in seamlessly, despite the dichotomy of styles.

James had travelled extensively in Europe but had still not come across anywhere to rival Fornalutx for its seductive combination of beautiful and dramatic setting, with its pine-clad mountains on three sides and views of the orange groves and neighbouring Soller in the valley below and the golden stone townhouses with their uniform green shutters, packed along ever steeper levels. The wide, mule-friendly steps were not for the faint-hearted but the views from the houses at the top of these steps overlooking the village and down the valley towards the sea, were stunning. James felt his choice of location for his new life ticked most of his boxes and sighed with an air of self-satisfaction.

His gaze returned to his empty glass and suddenly back to the itch he couldn't scratch, on seeing Steve's cigarette packet and lighter on the table. Thoughts of working out the complexities of the Steve issue subsided with a yawn. It would keep till morning, he thought. He lifted the cigarettes and lighter, took some money out of his pocket and paid Pepe, before walking the short distance up the steps to his house and to his bed.

The next morning James woke to the sound of squeaking window shutters being pulled back and the noise of chairs being moved on his roof terrace. He could hear his wife, Charlotte, already up serving break-fast to his two sons, Adam and Reuben. The full glory of the morning sun was still behind the Tramuntana Mountains but its rays were creeping over the valley, as a precursor to its full strength later in the day. The posi-tion of his bed gave him a clear view of the pine trees dotted all the way up to the top of the Puig Major, the highest peak in the range. His thoughts were halted as Charlotte walked in.

"I didn't hear you come in last night. Were you late?" she asked.

"I got in just after one," replied James.

"What's that?" demanded Charlotte in a schoolmis-tressy tone, pointing at the cigarette packet on James' bedside cabinet. Suddenly, his meeting of Steve and his uneasiness about him flooded back.

"They belong to a guy I met last night and he left them," said James in a matter of fact way.

"Yeah, yeah," said Charlotte in a slow sarcastic manner.

"Alright I did have one but they do belong to this guy Steve. He joined Matt, Jayne and me for a drink. He's just moved into the village."

"Where's he from?" asked Charlotte.

"Well the funny thing is he's from Bermondsey but he's not the sort of bloke you'd expect to buy a house here on his own."

"Why what's wrong with him?" she asked scornfully.

"Nothing... well it's just he comes across as if he's got a bit of form, if you know what I mean."

"You're awful!" said Charlotte in a playful way.

"Well anyway, I'll return them after breakfast. Are the boys up?"

"Of course," she replied.

"Right! Time to get up!" said James, throwing back the bed sheet and jumping up.

After a leisurely breakfast on the roof terrace with his family, James left his house armed with two bags of rubbish and a bag full of items for the recycling bank. On the way down the steps he suddenly remembered he would be going past what he believed was Steve's house but he had forgotten to bring the cigarettes and anyway he was half way down and his hands were full. I'll do it later, he thought as he studied the house he thought was Steve's as he walked past, looking for any sign of life or confirmation that it was indeed the right house. Through a partially glazed front door, he could see the outline of a dog, which barked on seeing him. That must be it, he thought as he continued on his way to the bin lorry to dispose of his rubbish.

He wandered up the hill from the bottle bank, slightly out of breath, as the mid morning sun blazed down from above, to the corner shop for a newspaper. The café's tables were already half full in the plaça. The relative peace was occasionally being disturbed by a cacophony of noise from a builder's drill at a nearby house, the whirring sound of a motorbike changing gears and passing cars navigating the tight bend which skirted the plaça.

James caught sight of Garth, a gregarious retired accountant from Australia.

"Good morning Garth," said James.

"Morning," replied Garth, lifting his head up from his newspaper with a smile. "Fancy a coffee?" he asked in his throaty Antipodean twang.

"Don't mind if I do," replied James, as he sat down at the table.

Garth beckoned Pepe. "Two café con leche please Pepe."

"Coming right up, Garth."

"Well, what have you been up to?" asked Garth, putting his newspaper down.

"Oh, just working on the house," said James. "I was here last night with Matt and Jayne, our Irish friends, whom you've met. You were conspicuous by your absence."

"Well Jenny and I had dinner with Catalina and it was my friend Terry's last night here. In fact, I'm just back from dropping him off at the airport."

Pepe returned with two coffees.

"Did your friend find you last night James?" asked Pepe, placing the coffees on the table.

"Who Steve?" said James.

"No, the one who came to the bar just after you went home last night. I've never seen him before but he asked for you by name and said he was a friend of yours. I told him you had just left and he asked where you lived. I said I didn't know which house but I knew it was up the steps," said Pepe.

"What did he look like Pepe?" asked a bemused James.

"I'd say he was about forty maybe, your build, dark hair and he spoke English like that new guy Steve. Maybe he was from London too, no?"

"Thanks Pepe," said James in a quiet, contemplative voice.

"Anything wrong?" asked Garth, looking perplexed.

"No, it's just a bit strange," said James. "I can't think for the life of me who that would have been. It doesn't describe anyone I can think of… unless it could have been a friend of Steve's?"

"Who's Steve?" asked Garth.

"He's a guy from London I met last night with Matt and Jayne. He's moved into the village. I think it's the house two up from Catalina."

"Oh that guy!" said Garth in a disdainful way, rolling his eyes. "Catalina says he plays loud music till three in the morning and his dog keeps shitting outside her house. I know who you mean. That guy's a bloody arsehole!"

"Well unless it's a friend of his and he sent him to get his cigarettes for him or something… anyway."

James drained his cup, "I'll leave you to finish your sudoku in peace. Thanks for the coffee. By the way are we still on for lunch on Tuesday?"

"Oh yeah, Jenny thought we'd just eat at Es Turo."

"Perfecto. See you later."

On returning home, James found Charlotte in the kitchen.

"Are you working next door today?" she asked. "It's just Adam has only got a week left before he starts his new school and I think you should spend some time with him."

"You're right. I'll give Tomeu a ring and tell him not to come today. He'll probably be at the Port in any case. Do you fancy the beach then?" asked James.

"Yes I think so," replied Charlotte. "Adam wants to try out his new bodyboard and Reuben is just happy playing in the sand, so yes."

Tomeu was James' Mallorcan builder and architect and a good friend, who along with James was transforming a wreck of a house next door to his own home into a small 'boutique' hotel, which Charlotte and James would run. James shared Tomeu's love of architecture and both enjoyed each other's company. James enjoyed listening to Tomeu recount stories of when he was a drummer touring with Julio Eglesias and of the rise and fall of the fortunes of his family's glass making factory and what life was like in the days of General Franco. Tomeu had told him stories of the atrocities that happened in Mallorca during The Spanish Civil War. Stories told to him by his father, where even the clergy were not spared. One story related to churches being set on fire after reports that priests were shooting at nationalist forces from the church towers. As a result of this a dozen priests were summarily executed, only for it to be discovered a week later that Republican soldiers had done the shooting from the belfries. The War was most brutal on the Spanish mainland and Mallorca did not see anything like the fighting that took place there. In fact Mallorca was captured without much of a struggle by the nationalists and became an important naval and air base for them for the duration of the war. Despite this, Tomeu recounted stories of bitter animosity even to this day of local neighbouring families who still won't forget what was done during that time.

Tomeu was a good man to know, as he was from an old Mallorcan family and his local knowledge was invaluable. He knew who was the best carpenter, where to go for the best food, if you had any questions with any form of bureaucracy he knew what or where or who to see and the fact that he spoke fluent English, having lived in Australia and being married to an Australian was a bonus.

"I'd better nip down and return these cigarettes," said James. "Back in a minute."

He reached the front door of the house and knocked. The dog behind the glazed door barked loudly. After a few moments he knocked again, whipping the dog inevitably into another frenzied barking fit. There was still no reply. He must be out, thought James and he turned from the front door to make his way back home, when suddenly something made him stop in his tracks. Nothing material, nor discernible, something more subtle, yet equally powerful. An instinct drew him back to the door. He pushed down on the door handle and the door opened. Slowly James pushed the door ajar only by a few inches, surprised to find it open and conscious that he did not want the fanged canine to think he was lunch. As he anticipated, the dog's nose peaked through the gap in the doorway, tentatively, frightened even; not with the ferocity that he had expected. He opened the door fully to reveal a brown mongrel, which immediately ran out past him but returned, sniffing all around him, licking James' nervously outstretched hand. As he patted the dog he could see a dark patch under the dog's chin. It looked like blood.

Had the dog injured himself? He thought.

James peered into the entrada of the house and called out;

"Hello! Steve, anyone home?"

He waited for a reply or some sign of stirring. None came. The entrada was in darkness save for the stream of light coming in through the open front door. He looked down on the pale coloured floor tiles and saw the pattern of numerous paw prints going to and from the front door and back to a room straight ahead with its door open but which remained in relative darkness. James bent down to look at the paw prints. He wiped one with his hand. It was dry to the touch but on looking at his fingers, his heart raced. It was blood.

2

CARPE DIEM

About five years earlier, it had been a clear, cloudless February morning when James had driven from Soller towards Fornalutx along the narrow twisting road which wound gradually upwards towards the village, passing fincas set in orange and lemon groves, the branches of which were heavily laden with fruit. The Soller valley still produced the oranges that had brought it wealth and a close connection with France. King Louis XIV would only have Soller valley oranges on his breakfast table and many of the merchants sought and made their fortunes in France before returning and giving the architecture of the area a distinct French influence.

As he turned a corner, skirting alongside the torrent, the village came into view in all its magnificent splendour, rising up like chunks of honeycomb inviting him ever closer. It was as beautiful and awe-inspiring as he remembered and his heart beat faster in anticipation of what would be, as he was to complete the purchase of a townhouse in this little oasis. He drove up into the heart of the village past the plaça, which was full of people equipped with stout walking boots, knapsacks and carbon sticks, enjoying a coffee before a sojourn into the Tramuntana Mountains which surrounded the village.

After parking the hire car James made his way to his base for the next two days: The Petit Hotel, one of four small hotels the village had to offer. Strolling down the cobbled street, lined with terracotta pots full of an abundance of healthy greenery, James realised that Fornalutx' title of the prettiest village in Spain was deserved. Its charms had certainly beguiled him, drawing him in like a siren.

It was certainly a meteoric change from inner city London and Belfast and from the high crime rate, adrenalin-charged policing that he had been used to and where he learned his craft. He had seen both the best and the worst of people over twelve years working in areas where paramilitaries had a strangle hold over the populous and where murder was common. Attending scenes of murder or pipe bomb attacks had become routine in a spiral of mindless sectarianism or more often than not due to inter-paramilitary rivalry, over power, drugs or money. James had felt there was more to life than this. He had tried to make a difference and had been dedicated, but the job he once loved had become frustrating and insidious. It was changing him and destroying his family life. Enough was enough. A change of career had proved to be the making of him and success followed in business allowing him the opportunity to fulfill his dream of owning a property in his beloved Fornalutx. Like many before him the glimpse of a better life in a sun-drenched oasis of calm had brought him to this 'hidden' Mallorca. Life here was uncomplicated, at a slower pace and here life could be lived, not merely be a treadmill existence.

Mallorca, for James, was an island of contrasts. It had long been a bastion for those of an artistic persuasion. In the nineteenth century, before Robert Graves, author of '*I, Claudius*' et al, made Deia his home, one commentator discovered the residents of that particular Mallorcan village were a 'strange mixture of artists, artisans, writers and bohemians from all quarters.' The rich and famous had made Mallorca their playground and since the 1960's, package holiday-makers had been coming in their droves. He had been searching for the alternative Mallorca and in the Soller valley he felt he had found it.

James checked into the hotel, which was located down a narrow cobbled street flanked by three storey townhouses. His pleasant room was made all the more special by a clear and unobstructed view of the pine clad mountains and the finca dotted valley below.

The next morning he met the exuberant American couple Bob and Linda from whom he was buying the townhouse.

"Good morning! Sleep well?" asked Bob with vigour.

"Yes, fine," replied James.

"Well this is it. All ready to take the plunge?" asked Linda.

"Let's do it," replied an enthusiastic James.

The three chatted in the car on route to Soller and to the notary's office. James had first to go to his bank to withdraw a sizeable sum of money, known as 'black money', which was to be paid to the Americans in cash during the proceedings in the notary's office. He initially was reticent to do this, but the practice of under-declaring the purchase price was the only way you can buy a property in Mallorca. Still James felt a little uneasy about carrying a large brown envelope stuffed with cash, even the short distance between the bank and the notary's office, but his journey was uneventful and he arrived to find his lawyer waiting for him.

During the proceedings the notary left the room for a short period to allow the hand-over of cash, returning to then finalise the name change on the deeds. Within an hour James was the proud new owner of a little piece of Mallorcan real estate.

Soller was the venue for a celebratory meal that evening courtesy of Bob and Linda at Ciprianni's Restaurant in Soller's plaça.

"Well, what would you like to drink?" asked Bob rubbing his hands.

"I think I'll have a beer while I'm deciding," replied James.

"I'll have a glass of vino tinto," said Linda, looking through the menu.

"This is nice!" said James. "I haven't been in here before."

The restaurant had black and white chequered tiles on the floor and had a French-Italianate look with a hardwood bar and a very intimate formal little dining room over-looking the plaça through French windows at the front of the more casual dining area.

"They do fantastic steaks here," said Bob. "I usually get one here as I don't eat meat that often, as Linda is a vegetarian."

"Do you mean to tell me Linda that you deprive this man of a good piece of meat at home?" said James in a tongue in cheek way.

"Bob is quite happy with a nice piece of fish but he does enjoy a good steak when we're out, although anything here is good," said Linda.

The drinks arrived at the table and Bob raised his glass:

"A toast to you James and your lovely family. I hope you have as much pleasure from the house as Linda and I have had. Cheers!"

"Cheers! Good health!" replied James.

The wine flowed and the pleasant conversation continued and the evening was rounded off back at James' newly acquired house with liberal measures of Old Bushmills whiskey.

Over the next few years James and his family spent many happy days holidaying in Fornalutx, making many good friends who had made the valley their home and soon James came to hanker after a more permanent move. It was all very well enjoying the island as a tourist for a week or so every few months but he wanted to integrate into society and to make Mallorca his home.

It was a long hard slog but James was a true believer in the adage 'carpe diem' and despite some setbacks he realised his dream and made the village his family's home. His plan was to renovate the house next to his and to convert it into a small 'boutique hotel' to provide a source of income and to be a springboard for him to convey to his guests his enthusiasm for the area.

He planned to spend a year working on the renovation project before opening, while his sons would be educated in the local school, in the case of his younger son, Reuben and one of the International schools for Adam and over time they should be bi-lingual. He enjoyed the satisfaction of bringing something back to its former glory, having renovated several homes from Georgian farmhouses to thatched cottages. So the Moorish wreck that he had bought beside his townhouse didn't seem too daunting.

Having arrived at the beginning of July he and his family planned to enjoy the summer before his sons started school, but James couldn't help starting the project, eager to see his new venture come to fruition. His days had so far been a mix of hard labouring on the building, combined with his parenting duties and taking his family to the beach at nearby Port de Soller, enjoying all that a Mallorcan summer had to offer.

Port de Soller, which had once been a small, traditional fishing village was now a bustling marina with a plethora of restaurants and hotels that mixed chic with the old world charm of a traditional bucket and spade beach holiday. Its golden sand beach at Repic on the eastern side of the horse–shoe bay was flanked on either side by two lighthouses, standing like sentries on guard. At the western end of the Port, traditional fishing boats sat comfortably cheek by jowl with sleek yachts and 'gin palaces'. The daily catch of the day being offloaded to be cooked in the many fine fish restaurants locally.

It was a place full of the hustle and bustle of holiday-makers enjoying the delights of a busy coastal resort, with the clatter and intermittent hooting of the horns from the antique trams, which made their way down the well-worn tracks from Soller, carrying locals and tourists alike.

Soller, a couple of kilometres inland, was the main town of the valley, a mixture of traditional stone townhouses interspersed with grand mansion houses; a result of the opulence the returning émigrés were keen to replicate from their days in Paris and beyond. It had at its centre a modernist church, the inspiration of one of Gaudi's pupils, with a plaça in front of it kept shaded by plane trees. This was often were James would bring his family to enjoy café society and indulge in a spot of people watching while his sons would happily play within the confines of the plaça. Soller, along with the neighbouring villages, played host to many fiestas throughout the year. Mallorca truly was a place for all seasons.

Over the first few weeks of his new life, James felt as if he was still on holiday. It was July and the tourist season was in full flow, but he still had to pinch himself that he was now 'living the dream', that this is where he would wake up in the morning, every morning and where he would go to bed at night. He felt that his boat had finally come in.

He decided the best way to overcome this feeling that he was still on holiday was to get stuck into the renovation work whilst still making time for his family. The house he was renovating required being taken back to its shell and practically rebuilt, with a new third floor extension and new roof, new luxurious bath-rooms, balconies and a small dipping pool was to be built in the rear enclosed courtyard. Care would have to taken to keep the soul of the building and compromises would have to be made, balancing keeping original features whilst discretely inserting modern necessities like air-conditioning and central heating.

He had to temper his penchant for hard graft and his enthusiasm for getting things done to the exclusion of everything else, against the fact that he had other commitments, namely his wife and sons and spending a portion of the day with them. This was a big move for all of them, perhaps even more so for his sons. Reuben was still young enough to adapt quickly in learning a new first language and getting to grips with a new climate, new school and new customs. Adam's transition may prove to take a little longer, as he was at a formative age and had left friends back in England and a schooling system that he was comfortable with and excelled in. James felt that the opportunities for Adam were just as good as in England and in many ways even better but he resolved to make the transition as smooth as possible which meant spending some quality father and son time with both the boys, so time management would be paramount.

3

DO NOT GO GENTLE

James cautiously walked into the entrada of Steve's house and called out once more,
"Hello! Steve! Anyone home?"

A wall of silence was his reply, save for the muffled barking of the dog, which had moved off further down the street. He took small steps hoping to be startled by a just wakened Steve, or for him to appear at the front door behind him, having been to the shop for a paper, wishful thinking though it was. He was drawn towards the darkened room ahead and with an acute sense of foreboding he continued. In the few seconds he had been in the dim entrada, his eyes were growing accustomed to the absence of light and as James entered the darkened room he could see the dark shape of a large object lying on the floor between a sofa and a coffee table. He could see the outline of the window on the wall opposite the door but the wooden shutters cut out the sunlight. He walked to the window, opened it and pushed back the green shutters, flooding the whole room with bright sunlight. James turned to see what the darkness would not give up.

In an instant his worst fears were realised. The room resembled the aftermath of a bar room brawl; overturned chairs, broken glasses and lamps and the motionless body of Steve. He assumed it was Steve, by the clothing he recalled him wearing from the previous evening. As he bent down over the body his heart beat faster. The body was lying on its front with a dark pool of blood around the head. He slowly gripped the torso under the right arm and pulled it backward, whilst checking for a pulse in the neck. He checked several times but in truth did not expect to find one, as on seeing the face covered in congealed blood and despite the severe swelling, he could identify this poor unfortunate as Steve the Londoner. It quickly became apparent that Steve was dead.

Instantaneously the faces of those victims whose bodies James had seen in similar violent circumstances, but had been conveniently deposited and filed in the deepest recess of his mind marked 'DO NOT OPEN', all left simultaneously and were appearing to him in quick succession.

The full enormity of the situation took a moment to register with James. It was not the realisation that Steve had been murdered that troubled him. The words of Dylan Thomas' poem came into James' head *"Do not go Gentle into that good night..."* and Steve had clearly not gone without a fight, judging by the state of the room and his face. What he was shocked by was not the apparent violence and brutality of the assault, the like of which he had seen before but the fact that it had happened here in Fornalutx, in the next street from his house. How could this happen under a Mallorcan sky?

A wave of despair and anger swept over him. Despair at man's inhumanity to his fellow man. He felt very aware of his own mortality just at that moment but this was quickly superseded by the more powerful feeling of anger at someone doing this in HIS village.

He quickly gathered his thoughts and returned to type. He went into automatic pilot without thinking. It was too late to preserve Steve's life but what about his? Was he in danger? Surely no one in their right mind would hang about after doing this but clearly the person responsible was not in their right mind.

He quickly checked the other rooms on the next two floors. Each room showed signs of having been disturbed, of something being searched for. Was this a burglary gone wrong? He returned to the ground floor room, satisfied there was no one else in the house.

His thoughts turned to scene preservation and alerting the authorities. He went to the front door and closed it to stop the dog from returning and adding to the chaos of the scene. It occurred to him that Steve may have known his killer. There was no sign of forced entry to the front door, which was the only access in or out. The house did not have a garden, only a small roof terrace on the third floor, which he had checked. In an instant it also occurred to him that he may have been the last person along with Matt to see Steve alive in the plaça, the previous night. What about the call he took on his mobile? It suddenly became more relevant. Who was the man who had asked for James at Café sa Plaça after he had gone to bed? Could he be connected? Questions ran through James' head but were quickly ousted by the realisation that he was in the middle of a stranger's house and that stranger was lying in a pool of his own blood – dead – having been brutally murdered without any apparent motive, in a foreign country, which although now his home, he suddenly felt outside of his comfort zone. He spoke virtually no Spanish, he was no longer a police officer and besides the Spanish police had never shaken off their reputation as, at best, uncompromising. How do you explain this? Could he be viewed as a suspect? Panic engulfed him momentarily. He had nothing to hide and for the sake of his fellow residents, if not for the sake of the unfortunate Steve, he had a duty to get the police there as soon as possible. The killer had had a good eight hours head start and may even have left the island by then.

James composed himself, took a deep breath and turned towards the front door. He opened it and stepped outside, closing the door behind him. He looked up and down the empty street. In the distance, he could see Steve's dog sniffing at the pavement. He walked towards the plaça and pulled his mobile phone from his pocket. On turning the corner, to his great relief, he saw Simon, a friend and owner of Café Med, ready to open up his restaurant. He bounded up to Simon, who appeared visibly startled by James' speed of approach.

"Simon! Thank God!" started James. "Listen carefully. I need you to ring the police. Did you know Steve the guy from London?"

"Yeah, he lives round the corner…"

"Well he's been murdered," interrupted James, "I've just come from his house. This is not a joke. Hurry, please do it now. I've got to make sure no one goes in."

Simon was dumb-founded and stared blankly at James before visibly snapping into action, "Right, well I'll do it now," and he turned quickly and went inside.

James went to the corner of the street from where he could see the front door of Steve's house, whilst staying within view of Simon's restaurant. A couple of minutes, which seemed like an eternity passed and still Simon had not reappeared.

"Simon! Any news?" demanded an agitated James.

An instant reply was not forthcoming which did not help James' stress levels. He reached into the pocket of his shorts in an effort to once again pull out his mobile phone but in his haste pulled out the cigarette packet instead. Pausing briefly to ponder whether it was right to smoke a cigarette belonging to a dead man James quickly surmised his need was justified and hastily took out a cigarette and lit it, which helped to calm him somewhat. Half a hurried cigarette later Simon reappeared from his restaurant. James motioned to him to join him.

"Well what did they say?" asked James hurriedly.

"I had to tell them several times before they realised I wasn't joking," said Simon. "They are sending police from Soller as quickly as they can and they said not to go back in. I can't believe it. Are you sure he's dead?" he asked hopefully.

"Simon believe you me if you saw the state of him, he's dead alright. I don't want to startle you but he's been badly beaten and he's definitely dead."

"Oh my God!" said Simon. "Have you just found him?"

"Yes. I only met the guy for the first time last night and I came to return his fags and there was no reply but his dog was barking so I went in and found him on the floor in his living room. The whole house is a mess. Did you know him?" asked James.

"Just to say hello to. I knew he had bought the house beside Catalina and I'd see him out walking his dog past the restaurant but that's about it. He has only been here a few weeks, if that. Shit, I can't believe this."

Simon shook his head in bewilderment.

"Someone doesn't do this sort of thing without a reason. It looks as if they were looking for cash or valuables or something! I don't know," sighed James. "What a mess. I thought I'd left all this sort of thing behind me," he continued.

"I don't feel like opening up now," said Simon, "and anyway this area will probably be full of police shortly," he continued.

In the distance James heard the faint sound of a siren, which as he listened was getting louder as it appeared to be heading in their direction.

"This could be them now," said James.

Sure enough, within seconds a police car came round the corner, stopped and two policemen got out and walked in the direction of James and Simon. James walked to meet them with Simon following a few steps behind.

The younger policeman greeted the two: "Bon dia. English?"

James replied, "Si."

"You call us?" he asked.

"My friend here did but I found the body. He is inside this house," said James pointing to the front door of Steve's house.

The two police officers turned and spoke to each other in Catalan. They walked to the door and pushed down on the handle and opened the door. The older one looked back at James and motioned for him to stay where he was. The two officers went inside tentatively and James saw the younger one place his hand on the handle of his holstered firearm.

"Hola! Hello!" shouted the men inside. They had left the front door ajar and James pointed towards the room at the end of the entrada, as the younger policeman glanced back towards him. Both men then disappeared from his view as they entered the room. Simon moved closer to James and craned his neck in an effort to see into the entrada.

"What's that on the floor?" he asked James.

"His dog must have been sniffing round the body. It's his dog's paw prints," replied James.

He could hear the sound of another siren heading in their direction.

"Sounds like reinforcements," said James.

Simon made no reply, still looking into the entrada for some sign of evidence of the macabre event. A few moments later the younger policeman reappeared from the room and walked outside. His mood was sombre and he looked visibly shaken. He spoke into his police radio just as a second police car came into view and another two members of the Policia Local alighted from their vehicle and walked towards them. The younger officer walked towards them and spoke to them in a volley of rapid words like a machine gun firing on automatic. One of the new arrivals motioned with his hand for the younger man to slow down, whilst looking James up and down. After what appeared to be a never-ending monologue, the younger officer turned and pointed at James and the two other police officers walked towards him.

"Hello. I am Miguel Santore, head of the police in Soller. My officer tells me you found the dead man," said one of the policemen to James.

"Yes. I found him about half an hour ago. I then asked my friend here to call the police," replied James.

"What is your name please? Do you live in Fornalutx?" asked the officer.

"My name is James Gordon and I live in Carrer San Sebastia," replied James.

The officer accompanying this man started writing in his notebook.

"You will stay with this man, yes?" asked the police Chief pointing to his colleague as he and the younger officer went into the house.

"Of course," replied James.

A few minutes later and the police Chief emerged and spoke to his colleague in Catalan before turning to James.

"Who was the man?" he asked.

"All I know is his name was Steve. He originally came from London and he moved to the village about a few weeks ago. I met him at Café sa Plaça last night for the first time. He got a phone call on his mobile phone and he said he was going home but stated he would come back in ten minutes. That was about 11.30pm. By one o'clock he had not returned so I went home to bed. He left his cigarettes behind, so this morning I came to return them to him. I knocked but there was no reply. I found the door was unlocked so I went inside. I noticed the blood on the floor and on his dog, which was barking and I went into the room at the end of the entrada and found him lying there as you see him. I lifted him slightly to check for a pulse but it was clear he was dead," said James.

The Chief looked James up and down and then said, "You will come to the police station, yes?"

"Of course," replied James.

"We go now," said the Chief.

James turned to Simon and said, "Simon can you go to my house and tell Charlotte what's happened? Tell her not to worry and I'll ring her as soon as I can."

"Yes no problem. I'll go now," he said walking in the direction of James' street.

James turned and walked with the Chief and the other officer in the direction of their car. The officer opened the rear door and James got in. A sinking feeling came over him. He felt strange getting into the rear seat of the police car as some tourists passed by, looking at him with contempt, as if he had just been arrested.

The Chief continued to ask James questions during the short journey to the police station in Soller and James could see him watching him in the mirror of his sun visor, which he had pulled down.

On arrival at the police station he was shown into a room and told to sit at the table. The other police officer stayed with him but it became clear that either he did not speak English or he didn't want to engage in conversation with him. He sat in the small room at a table going over the events of that morning and of the night before in an effort to see if he had missed any crucial element that might shine some light on what had happened. He kept coming back to what Pepe had told him about a man who had come to the bar after he had gone to bed. It was definitely not someone he knew and why would he be looking for him at that time of night? Pepe knew most, if not all of James' friends locally and he did not know the man. He came to the conclusion that this man was either the killer or was linked to the murder, but that still begged the question of why he would be looking for James. He didn't know Steve but he did feel that whoever had killed him appeared to have been looking for something. You don't ransack a house unless you are looking for something. Steve was a big guy and it would have taken more than one person to inflict the sort of injuries he had sustained and to kill him in the manner he had been killed. James felt he must have been held down by at least two, strong men before the final 'coup de grace'. Could Steve have told James something that was important to these men without James realising it? He tried to remember the extent of their conversation but it had just been small talk and all he had found out from Steve was that he was originally from Bermondsey in southeast London. He remembered the cigarettes and lighter that Steve had left. The lighter was just a cheap disposable one and it was just an ordinary cigarette packet. He put his hand into his pocket and brought out the box of Marlboro Lights and looked at the packet for anything unusual. Nothing. He looked inside. There were nine or ten cigarettes left and he lifted a handful of four of five out. James froze. There was something inside. He looked up at the policeman who was watching him.

"No smoking," he said abruptly.

At least James knew then that 'Mr Cheerful' spoke English. James peered into the packet and could see something metallic. It was a key. He put the other cigarettes back in the packet and returned them to his pocket. His mind raced. Why would you conceal a key at the bottom of a cigarette packet? Is this what they were looking for? Was Steve killed because of this key? What was it the key to? He ached to open the packet and study the key in detail but some sense of not wishing to disclose this kept him from doing just that.

The door to the room suddenly opened and the Chief entered the room with a stocky man in an open-necked shirt. The Chief spoke to the uniformed officer who had been guarding James, who then left the room. The Chief sat down at the other side of the table with the stocky man. He was in his early forties with a shaved head and stubble and was staring right at James, which made him uncomfortable. He was after all, merely a witness, helping the police with their enquiries and a former police officer to boot. If they were attempting to play the Spanish version of 'good cop, bad cop' he was not having it. He returned the unflinching stare of the stocky cop but deflected his gaze when the Chief addressed him.

"This is Inspector Martinez from the serious crime department of La Policia Nacional. He will be leading the investigation into the murder of the Englishman in Fornalutx. We need to know where you were last night and who you were with," said the Chief.

"I was with two friends called Matt and Jayne Smith in the plaça from about ten o'clock. I went to the toilet and returned to my table to find the guy Steve there. I chatted to him for about an hour and a half. He was from a part of London I knew, as I had been a policeman there about fifteen years ago. He got a call on his mobile and said he had to go home but said he would be back. That was about 11.30pm. My friends Matt and Jayne had both left by 1am and I left shortly after. Pepe, the barman can confirm this. I had never met this man Steve before last night and my wife will confirm that I returned home just after 1am. I was only made aware that he had moved to Fornalutx and bought the house where I found him, by him, last night. He left his cigarettes at the table last night, so this morning I went to return them to him, which is when I found him."

The stocky Inspector then spoke,

"This is a peaceful island and it is not usual to have something like this happen. It is only when you English come here or the South Americans that we have trouble, so if there is anything you are not telling us it will be bad for you."

James looked directly at the Inspector, surprised at how good his English was before replying,

"For a start I am from Northern Ireland; I am not English and secondly I did not have anything to do with the murder of that man. What I have told you is the truth and if you suspect otherwise then I demand to speak to a lawyer."

James was conscious of the fact that he had not told them about his recent discovery of the key and for some reason he didn't feel inclined to do so, at least not at that moment, anyway. He also thought to himself how different this was to evidence gathering in the UK, if what he had just experienced was a formal interview. There was no legal representation, no video recording nor tape recording and in fact neither man had written down a single word.

"We will release you on one condition," said the Inspector, "that you surrender your passport at the police station until we can eliminate you from the inquiry. You will do this?" he asked.

James thought about it and was going to acquiesce just to get out of there, but then he thought why should he give this up? He wasn't sure of his rights in this situation in Mallorca but it seemed that unless he was a suspect and had been given legal advise or allowed the opportunity to speak to the consulate, he did not want to hand over his passport.

"No I don't agree to that. I am here voluntarily helping you and if I am to be treated as a suspect you must tell me that is the case. I have no plans to leave the island and you have my address. If I had something to do with the murder do you think I would hang around and report it?" said James, getting a little agitated at the possibility they were considering him as a suspect.

Both men stood up and left the room, to be replaced by his former guard. James suddenly recalled his only other experience of being in a foreign police station, many years ago in Lyon, France. He was 14 years old and had gone with his family to visit his sister who was studying there. On one particular day a friend of his sister took him into the city centre by bus. James had purchased a 'carnet' of bus tickets but it became apparent that his companion had doctored his ticket, ending in James and his companion being taken to a city centre police station. Whilst there he witnessed the assault of a prisoner in handcuffs by police, which left an indelible mark in his mind, giving him the impression that police in other European countries may not quite follow the good practice of UK policing. He knew how to handle himself but he did not want to be a statistic on a 'death in custody' file.

A short time later the Inspector returned by himself.

"Ok. I will allow you to go but I need your phone number and if you are leaving the island you must inform me personally. In the meantime I will be speaking to the barman and to your friends. If you remember anything else you can ring me on this number," he said handing James a card.

James left and rang his wife to tell her to pick him up as he walked towards Soller's main square. He deposited himself at a table outside one of the many cafés that surround the square and ordered a beer. He then produced the cigarette packet from his pocket, took one out and lit it, whilst reaching inside the box for the key, which he retrieved. It was a small key on a green fob with the number 27 on the fob. It was too small to be a house key, thought James but there was nothing else to indicate where it was from or what it was for. He held it in his hand hoping for inspiration and pondering whether he should go straight back to the police station and inform the Inspector of his discovery. James was intrigued and realised his interest in solving crime had never left him. He decided to try and investigate this further himself and if nothing further could be established he would hand over the key to the Inspector as soon as possible.

A short time later Charlotte, James' wife arrived with his sons. She came straight up to him and hugged him.

"Are you alright? I was so worried when Simon told me," she said.

"I told you on the phone I'm alright," replied James.

"I know but I can't believe this. So what exactly did you find?" asked Charlotte sitting down.

"Adam take Reuben over there and have a run about for five minutes," said James.

"Ok I will but could we maybe get an ice-cream?" Adam asked hopefully.

"I'll get you one when you come back, so off you go," said James, turning to Charlotte.

"I'll spare you the gory details but it's true the guy has been murdered and that's about it. I have no idea why but I told you this morning that I felt uneasy about him. I'm going to see if I can find anything out about him from CID in Rotherhithe. I have no doubt police will know him. There is one thing though... I think whoever did it was looking for something. I have just found this in his cigarette packet," said James producing the key from his pocket, showing it to Charlotte.

She leaned forward to view the key and picked it up and examined it closely.

"This was in his cigarette packet?" she asked looking puzzled.

"Yes I only discovered it when I was in the police station. It may not have anything to do with this but why would you keep a key in your fag packet? And it was hidden under the cigarettes, which is why I didn't notice it before."

"It looks like a locker key," said Charlotte.

"Could be. I doubt it was for his locker at his Country Club," said James raising his eyebrows.

"What did the police think?" asked Charlotte, handing the key back.

"Well I haven't told them yet," replied James.

"Why on earth not?" asked a perplexed Charlotte.

"I don't know," said James sheepishly. "Look I only found it an hour ago and I've only just thought it might be relevant and anyway I didn't like the attitude of the police. They were treating me as if I had something to do with it."

James looked at Charlotte who was frowning at him.

"I know! I know! You're right. I should tell them and I will. It's just... I think because it's happened in our village and because I was the last person perhaps to see him alive, that I feel obliged to try and find who did this," said James.

"Don't be ridiculous!" exclaimed Charlotte. "A man has been murdered. You're not a policeman any more and this is Mallorca. We're not at home now; well you know what I mean. I need you, your sons need you. This is dangerous, so stop messing about and leave it to the local police."

"Ok! Ok!" cried James. "Well anyway are you still up to going to the beach?" he asked.

"I think we should. The boys are keen to go and the village is full of police. There was even a TV camera crew outside his house when we were leaving," said Charlotte.

"Adam! Reuben! Come on we're going now," called James.

A short drive from Soller led them to the Port de Soller and to the beach. James parked the car and the family alighted and loaded each other up like pack horses with beach towels, mats, sun cream, buckets and spades, beach balls and other items necessary to occupy two boys. The sun loungers were already almost fully occupied and the beach attendant had placed 'Reserved' signs on many others, but they managed to get three sun beds towards the promenade. James went to the elderly beach attendant, whose skin was a mahogany colour from day after day spent in the sun and paid for the beds. He returned to find Charlotte liberally applying high factor sun cream to both Adam and Reuben.

"Daddy, why were the Police in the village today and why were you at the Police station?" asked Adam inquisitively.

"Well," started James, pausing to find the words to best describe what had happened in a way not to alarm his son but without keeping the truth from him. James felt that it was wrong to wrap his son completely in cotton wool. He would have to make his own way in the world and be aware of its dangers but was this the right time to be explicit?

"Unfortunately something bad happened last night in the village, Adam. A man was killed and I found him, so I was helping the Police try and find who was responsible," said James looking at Adam for a sign of reaction, which he got instantaneously.

"Killed in Fornalutx?" said Adam concerned, "Who was it?"

"It's no one you knew, so don't worry. This sort of thing has never happened in the village before and is unlikely to happen there again. Sometimes people do bad things and it looks as if it might have been someone from back home who was responsible. It wasn't someone from the village. Look, do you remember when I was in the Police when you were very young in Northern Ireland?" asked James.

"Yeah kind of," replied Adam.

"Well back then this sort of thing happened some-times and we always got the person responsible," said James trying to reassure his son, but with only about a 30% murder clearance rate, was being somewhat economic with the truth.

James had attended numerous murder scenes in his former career and he had been on numerous murder investigation teams. His thoughts momentarily returned to those days. He enjoyed the camaraderie that life at the sharp end of policing in difficult and sometimes dangerous circumstances offered. He felt that an essential requirement to do that job was optimism and a dry sense of humour, which without one or both, sent some of his former colleagues on a downward spiral of alcohol abuse and depression.

"Anyway, don't concern yourself with that now," said James, getting back to the present. "It's a gorgeous day and I want to get into the water."

"Dad could we maybe swim out to the platform?" asked Adam, referring to a pontoon about 100 feet into the bay used as a diving platform.

"No problem but let's leave it until Reuben has had a splash in the sea. OK?"

"OK, that's fine."

After a while playing with both his sons in the water, James and Adam swam out to the pontoon and spent half an hour diving and bombing into the sea from the floating platform, working up quite an appetite in the process. After swimming back to shore he relaxed, prostrate on his sun lounger, recovering from his activity and drying off in the full heat of the midday sun.

"Anyone fancy some tapas for lunch?" he enquired.

"Yes. Are we going to 'Es Passeig'?" asked Charlotte.

"Yeah, it's the best I think."

The family walked the short distance along the promenade to the German-owned restaurant overlooking the beach and took a seat outside.

"Will I order the usual?" asked James.

"Yes and get some patatas fritas as well please," said Adam.

The waitress came to take the order.

"Could we have some boquerones, gambas, cala-mares, croquetas, albondigas and patatas fritas por favour?" said James in broken Spanish.

He relaxed over a cold beer and tried to put the events of the previous few hours out of his mind but they were all pervasive. It was impossible to sweep something like this under the carpet. He couldn't think clearly. Random thoughts were splurging out and not making sense like some abstract Jackson Pollock paint-ing. Could his Mallorcan dream be over before it had begun? For a few moments James pondered the idea of selling up and moving back to the UK. He was trying to think rationally. People are people no matter where you live. Some are good and some are capable of truly evil deeds, albeit that some have the propensity for more violence in certain parts of the world, more than in others and anyway he had no desire to move again. No, thought James, gathering his thoughts and achiev-ing some clarity of vision. This deed was probably an unwanted import from the UK, an act of violence prob-ably by a non-Mallorcan on a non-Mallorcan. It was most likely to be explained by the adage, 'those who live by the sword, die by the sword.' James' gut told him that the victim was no angel but no matter whoever he was or whatever he had done he certainly didn't deserve to die in that way. This was atypical of Mallorca let alone his village, so the more he thought about it, the more he resolved not to be forced, because of circum-stances, to leave the village and the paradise island that he now thought of as home.

James had seen first hand what was, for all intents and purposes, ethnic cleansing in parts of Northern

Ireland on both sides of the political and religious divide. It was a beautiful country, with the majority living in peaceful co-existence and harmony, but there were clearly those who could not live with people whose traditions or religion were slightly different to their own. The religious element of the issue was one that made James despair. For a start, those involved in sectarian violence for the most part hadn't darkened the door of a church in their lives and in a world of so many beliefs and religions for those who believed in the same God how could minor things like transubstantiation, the importance of the Virgin Mary and the issue of absolution, get in the way of people living peacefully together. Any other argument over it being a class struggle didn't hold water as it was usually the working classes on both sides who bore the brunt of the sectarian violence and as James had discovered first hand 'The Troubles' in Northern Ireland may have started out of frustration at inequality but this was no longer the situation and had become simply terrorists with their own agendas, bent on imprisoning their own people in a blanket of fear, whilst carrying out acts of terrorism or violence under a 'new flag of convenience' or due to in-fighting between their own kind when feuds came about. All this due to their own greed for power, money and some twisted sense that they represented 'their people' but usually were involved in drug-dealing, extortion and general criminality.

The so called Loyalists adopted such an uncompromising stance on their traditions and an unwavering allegiance to the Crown which James found confusing. This loyalty you might expect from former members of the Bullingdon Club in Her Majesty's Government, or the upper echelon of society, but not working class people from impoverished, grim estates. This loyalty did not extend to whatever party was in Government and Unionist politicians were more than happy to emulate their forerunners and play 'The Orange Card' to their advantage to extract any concession in exchange for their backing.

James felt saddened by the hopelessness that some found themselves in through poverty and circumstance. He had met a lot of truly genuine and selfless people in some of the worst areas of Belfast, unable to do anything about the grip the paramilitaries had over their respective communities. He recalled how one community worker from The Shankill Road in Belfast had said to James, when asked why he didn't move to a better area, free from paramilitary control,

"You need a Golden Ticket for that gig and I've had my fill of Wonka bars."

James later heard that the same worker managed to get out of the area but at a price. He had narrowly escaped with his life after his home suffered a petrol bomb attack as it was claimed he was, as the graffiti on his wall indicated, a 'police tout'. His wife was not so lucky in getting out and died of smoke inhalation. Just another pointless casualty.

The remainder of the day was enjoyed by the whole family and on returning home James rang Matt and told him what had happened. Matt arranged to meet James at Fornalutx later that evening, evidently shocked by the news.

James had found it difficult to relax at the beach and as they drove back up the main road to Fornalutx – known locally as 'the American Road', it had been built by the Americans and it led to a listening station used during 'The Cold War' – he suddenly felt a need to speak to Pepe again. What had begun to play on his mind was the fact that he could be putting his family in danger. It occurred to him that a killer was on the loose and potentially was looking for the key.

As they drove into the village James spotted Pepe and went over to speak to him.

"Pepe have you heard what's happened?" asked James.

"Yes the police spoke to me this afternoon and they asked if you were here last night. I can't believe it! I served him last night and now he's dead! This should not happen here!" said Pepe, who seemed genuinely distressed.

"Pepe do you remember the man who came to the bar looking for me last night? I want you to think very carefully and describe him to me," said James slowly.

"Let me think. He was maybe thirty-five years old, about your height and had muscles you know how you say... stocky. He had dark hair but it was short. Like I said to you, he spoke like that guy Steve," replied Pepe.

"Ok that's good. What was he wearing?" asked James.

"Oh I can't remember. Dark clothes; maybe. I didn't take much interest. Do you think he had something to do with this?"

"I don't know. Are you sure you've never seen him before? Do you know my friend Charlie from Soller? It wasn't him was it?"

"No, I know Charlie. It wasn't him. I see him all the time!" said an animated Pepe.

"Think back. What exactly did he say to you?"

"He came straight up to me and said 'have you seen James? I am a friend of his.' I said that you had just gone home and he asked where you lived. I said it was up the steps but I didn't know exactly which house and then he walked up the steps. I didn't see if he turned into your street or went straight on up because someone was paying their bill. That's all I can say."

"Ok Pepe. That's fine. Don't worry, the police will find who did this. Are you ok?" asked James considerately.

"Yes I suppose. It's not good for business though. I see you later James."

James returned home passing by Steve's house, which now showed no sign of the horrific scene that had greeted him only a few hours earlier, other than some police tape which now sealed the front door marking it as a crime scene. He enjoyed an uneventful dinner with his family, after which he rang Matt to cancel him coming to see him that evening. James felt emotionally drained and was in a reflective mood. He felt the best medicine for such an eventful day was a good night's sleep.

4

THE CASTELL D'ALARO

James awoke with a stream of golden light coming through a gap in his bedroom curtains. He stretched, yawning and looked at the clock on his bedside cabinet, which read 7:24. Charlotte stirred.

"Good morning," she yawned.

"Morning. Did you sleep alright?" enquired James.

"Fine. How are you feeling?"

"Oh I needed that. Right! Do you fancy going to the restaurant on the way to the Castel D'Alaro for lunch?" asked an enthusiastic James.

"Maybe."

"I fancy some of their roast suckling pig and I thought we could see if Matt, Jayne and the boys might like to join us. We could go for a walk before lunch up there, before it gets too hot and work up an appetite."

"Yeah why not?" replied Charlotte, getting out of bed, drawing back the curtains and allowing the full rays of the early morning sun to fill the room.

"Right then. I'll give them a ring after breakfast," said James, trying to sound cheerful in an effort to not let the events of the previous day become all-pervading.

The family breakfasted on the roof terrace, which afforded a view over the terracotta rooftops to the mountains and the valley below. The pretty hamlet of Biniaraix was easily discernable in the near-distance by the distinctive peaked church tower at its centre. The morning was resplendent in its full glory and as the village awoke to another cloudless day, the mood at breakfast was contented and jovial. James had only another week before Adam started at his new school and although Adam was a sociable, well-contented young man, James couldn't help feeling both excited and nervous for him, as he was about to be thrust into a new environment. He wanted to spend some quality father and son time with him but he would be able to do this later in the week. Today Adam would enjoy the company of Matt's boys and just hanging out with everyone.

James set off with his family in tow, mid- morning. The drive took them past Soller and through the long tunnel, which cut into the mountain, from which they emerged just before the Mallorcan town of Bunyola. A short distance further through the fertile Mallorcan countryside brought them to the delightful town of Alaro and high above it the ruins of a once fortified castle, which had been the backdrop to many incursions and battles between the Moors and Christians. James drove, admiring the bougainvillea-clad fences and the Mallorcan sandstone townhouses on either side of the road. He parked the car and stepped out, feeling the heat of the day instantaneously.

"Right get plenty of sun cream on boys," said James opening the boot of the car.

"Matt, Jayne and the boys should be here any minute and the table is booked for 1.30pm."

A short time later their friends arrived and the ritual 'creaming up' of parents and children alike was once again underway.

"Right everyone ready? We're just going up past the restaurant to the first viewpoint and back down, so you boys don't go too far ahead," shouted James to the four boys who were already at a gallop, heading up the steep incline which led up the mountainside.

Charlotte and Jayne walked either side of Reuben holding a hand each, occasionally swinging him backwards and forwards, which was accompanied by the 'weeeeing' sound of a contented toddler.

James and Matt hung back, observing the satisfying picture of contented wives and children, while they got down to the more demure subject of the murder.

"How are you feeling?" asked Matt.

"It doesn't get any easier seeing things like that. You think you become numbed by seeing so many gnarled and mutilated bodies and I suppose you do, but to find him like that in the village, I have to say it shocked me."

"So have the police any suspects or know why he was killed?"

"They appear to be more in the dark than we are. I meant to ask you, you know the first time you met Steve in Soller, I think you said he was with Brad. Was he with anyone else that night?"

"No. Brad and he came over and I had a couple of drinks with them, but I left them to it. I got the impression they were on more than just alcohol. As you know that eejit Brad likes his 'charlie'."

"Yeah I'm wondering if drugs had anything to do with this. The guy looked as if he had a bit of form. I'm going to call in a favour with a mate of mine who's in the CID in Rotherhithe, so I'll find out just who this guy Steve was. You know that the police in Soller interviewed me? I think they weren't sure what to make of my involvement and I think I could be a suspect as far as they're concerned."

"Well I got a call from them yesterday, I've to call at the police station after work tomorrow. So I'll put you in the frame for it, shall I?" asked Matt, smiling.

"Listen, don't even joke about it," said James, mustering a forced smile. "If I tell you something you've got to promise me not to mention it to them tomorrow."

"Sounds ominous," said Matt.

"Well do you remember I asked Steve for a cigarette and then he left?"

"Yes and that was the last we saw of him."

"Yes, well while I was at the police station I looked in the cigarette packet and saw he had hidden a small key inside. Charlotte thinks it might be a locker key or something. I think it might be important because every room in the house was ransacked and then a guy came looking for me later that night, who I told you about on the phone. I've checked with Pepe. It's nobody I know. I think Steve might have told his killer he didn't have the key and told him where it was; with his cigarettes with me and he's been killed regardless."

"So what don't you want me to tell the police?" asked a bemused Matt.

"I haven't told them about the key yet. I feel the urge to try and find out what it's for. Look it might have absolutely nothing to do with it and it could be the key to… to his bike chain for all I know. So I'm not asking you to lie. It would be hearsay anyway. Just don't mention it tomorrow. I will tell them but I am going to try and find out a bit more."

"Well it's your funeral but whatever you say Sherlock!"

"Who have you to see tomorrow anyway?"

"I can't remember. I have it written down. Hey do you think they'll give me the third degree? If you believe what Tomeu says about the Guardia Civil and they haven't changed much since Franco and nor have La Policia Nacional. Mind you, he thinks that's a good thing. He says crime was low in Franco's days... because everyone was shit scared to step out of line."

"Oh si senor, we are going to 'slap on the old brace-lets', give you a right good spankin' and how you say, stitch you up like a kipper!" said James grinning, slipping between a Spanish and cockney accent.

Matt laughed.

"I don't know about you but I could eat a buttered donkey! Will you be partaking in a couple of sherbets this afternoon?"

"Oh I think it would be rude not to," replied James.

"Mind you I'd better take it easy. I haven't fully recovered from last week. I told you about the Indian in Palma. It's superb. I wouldn't get the fahl again. It was a bit too hot. I had an arse like a Japanese flag all the next day!" laughed Matt.

"By the way, do you have the key with you?" asked Matt.

James brought the key out of his pocket and handed it to Matt. Matt looked closely at it before saying;

"Do you want me to take it to a friend of mine who's a locksmith. He could tell you what sort of a key it is."

"Thanks but I can't afford to lose this thing," said James, retrieving it from Matt's hand.

"Whatever you think," said Matt.

"How are things with the business?" asked James.

"Oh you know, not great but something will turn up," replied Matt.

As they reached the viewpoint, the siblings had already started their descent back towards the restaurant.

"Right boys see you down there. You can order yourselves a drink when you get there. We'll see you shortly," said James as they passed.

"Yeah dad we know," grunted Adam, pretending to be a disgruntled teenager.

"Soon he'll be talking like that for real!" laughed Matt.

James took out his prescription sunglasses from his pocket and scanned the view from left to right.

"Wow this is totally awesome!" he said in his best American accent.

He breathed in deeply. It was a truly breathtaking view, he thought. As he looked towards the horizon, he could make out Palma in the distance. In every direction he had a different vista. On one side he had the tranquillity of the mountains and on the other the valleys below. Beyond that, the honey-coloured settlement of Alaro and the rich ochre-coloured soil gave up its healthy bounty of oranges, lemons, olives and pomegranates. In the sky James noted the dark expansive wings of a bird of prey gliding on the currents the gentle breeze, effortlessly rising and falling over the plain.

"Look up there," pointed James.

"That looks like a black vulture," said Matt enthusiastically.

James felt like the master of all he surveyed. It was inspirational, he thought. The landscape showed little sign of the ravages of modern man and even the earthy tones of the houses were in harmony with their environment. The only sound was the gently swaying branches in the breeze and the constant low chirping of the cicadas and the occasional deep tinkling of a goat's bell as it manoeuvred across the mountainous terrain.

"I could stay here all day but my stomach has other ideas. Venga vamonos!" cried James.

They made their descent with a greater measure of vigour in anticipation of some honest home cooked food that the restaurant was famous for. Arriving at their rustic venue they deposited themselves under a vine-clad pergola and joined the 'four amigos' in a refreshing and well-deserved iced drink. Whilst the four boys engaged in a game of cards, observed intently and longingly at close quarters by the youngest of the brood, the adults scoured the menus.

"Anyone having a starter?" asked Matt.

"Well the portions here are huge but I think I might have some pa amb oli, while we're waiting. Fancy some?" asked James.

"Yes order some for everyone," replied Charlotte.

Pa amb oli is a traditional mallorcan peasant's dish that means quite literally bread with oil. It could be quite dry but James enjoyed the restaurant's interpretation of it with their rustic bread covered in olive oil and crushed garlic with sweet local tomato rubbed across the bread infusing it with colour and flavour.

"Have you tried the roast suckling pig here?" asked James.

"I haven't but Jayne has," replied Matt.

"It is so tender and full of flavour and the crackling… I never knew pork could be so tasty. Well I know what I'm having," said James, putting down his menu to observe the card game.

"You are a good salesman. I'll have the same," said Matt.

"Me too. It's just too good," said Jayne

"Oh well, I'll have to see what all the fuss is about. I'll have it too," said Charlotte.

"Oh we need a bottle of the 'Macia Batle' to go with that. Boys do you know what you want yet?" asked James.

"Roast chicken please," came the reply in unison.

The terrace of the restaurant quickly filled and James enjoyed a relaxing lunch with his friends and family well into late afternoon. Both families then bad farewell and set off for home, heading back into the Soller valley and then up the winding road that leads to Fornalutx.

The plaça was full of people enjoying the ambiance and just relaxing. Three of the village's elderly widows were sitting on a seat by the water fountain in the shade of a plane tree watching the comings and goings, while a toddler chased a ginger cat with utter delight across the square.

"Dad I see Enrique and Sarah, so I'm going to play with them in the square for a while, if that's OK," said Adam.

"Ok, but come up at about six o'clock," replied James.

As the evening wore on James decided to counter the excesses of his calorie intake and go for a run. He set off out of the village at the northern end up the twisting road which brought him onto the 'American road', which then descended, spiralling down the mountain-side, eventually bringing him out between Soller and its port. He decided to tackle the route heading back the way he had come, being much the greater trial on the ascent. The climb was arduous and James was soaked in sweat.

'No pain no gain,' he thought as he stopped briefly to catch his breath and admire the panoramic view, through the pine trees, of Soller below. He continued back up the ever-steeper climb until the road veered off in the direction of Fornalutx, having reached the peak, he exhaled slowly having completed the hardest part of the run. 'All downhill from here,' he thought, relieved that the worst of the six-kilometre run was now behind him. A group of lycra-clad cyclists flew past him on their descent towards the village giving him a wave in recognition of his efforts. Just as they had disappeared from view, he detected the sound of a car behind him some distance away. He looked back to see a silver coloured saloon type car about 50 yards behind him travelling at walking speed in his direction. James continued running unconcerned, as this was normal practice for drivers taking in the breath-taking views of the village and valley below. It was only when the vehicle continued at that speed and distance from him over the next half a kilometre that he began to pay some attention to it. Without his glasses James could not make out how many occupants the car had.

The sun was beginning to set behind the high peaks of the mountains and as he continued towards the village, the car suddenly raced past him and went out of sight round one of the twisting bends leading down towards the village. As it did so, he noted that the driver was its only occupant. The driver, a man of about 40 years of age, looked at him. He had short dark hair and wraparound sunglasses but it was his driving that concerned James. As he turned the next corner he could see the car had pulled off the road and was sitting with the engine switched off on a rough patch of ground by the side of the road. He felt uneasy. From the little he saw of the driver he felt that it could fit the description of the man whom Pepe had described. Could he be running headlong towards the potential murderer of Steve? He stopped, pretending to be admiring the view and started doing some stretching exercises whilst straining to see if the man was still in the driver's seat. Unable to make out if he was or not, he cursed his eyes but decided not to take any chances and slowly jogged back the way he had come, knowing he could divert down a dirt track that would bring him down into the village along another route. As he ran, speeding up, he looked back to try and get a glimpse of the car through the trees to see if it was following him. It had moved off but his view was obstructed and he couldn't see in what direction it had gone. He had to get home as quickly as possible, just in case. If it was the suspect it wouldn't take him long to get to his pedestrianised street. The guy had been told by Pepe the area where he lived, but not the house, it wouldn't take him long to find out if he asked the right people, although people in the village would be more suspicious of questions in light of what had happened.

James reached the far end of his cobbled street, stopped at the corner and peered round it. The coast was clear. He made it to his front door and went inside immediately, locking the door behind him. He switched off the light in the entrada and climbed the stairs. Charlotte was in the living room on the first floor and he entered the room that overlooked the street below. He switched off a lamp near the window and put his finger to his mouth in a gesture for her to be quiet and carefully opened the French windows and poked his head out just sufficiently to be able to see up and down the street to observe anyone entering his street.

"Can you get me my glasses?" he whispered to Charlotte.

"Yes, but what's going on?" she said concerned.

"Probably nothing but I just want to make sure," he replied in a soft voice without deflecting his gaze from the street below.

Charlotte returned and handed him his glasses, which he quickly put on and to his relief, his clarity of vision was fully restored.

James stood in silence; motionless, watching for about twenty minutes, observing only Marta and Magdelena, his neighbours returning from an evening stroll during this time. He quietly closed the French windows and pulled the curtains and slumped into a sofa, exhaling as he did so, somewhat relieved that the driver had not appeared.

"What was that all about?" asked Charlotte anxiously.

"I don't think it was anything. It's just when I was coming back along the top road a silver car was driving very slowly behind me and then it sped off. It just spooked me a little."

"I can see that. Look, would you for goodness sake go to the police tomorrow and give them that bloody key and tell them about the guy who came looking for you? What if that was him? What if he is looking for you and that key? You could be in danger. We all could be in danger. Oh great, I'm not going to sleep tonight."

"Are the boys in bed?" asked James.

"Yes. Is the front door locked?" asked Charlotte sharply.

"Yes it is, look don't worry. I will go to the police station tomorrow and sort it out. Ok?" he said giving Charlotte a hug.

"Ok. Well anyway I'm off to bed. Are you coming?"

"I'm going to have a quick shower and then I'll be up."

He went to bed a short time later but found it difficult to sleep, straining to hear any noise outside in the street below. He eventually fell asleep only to wake the next morning somewhat sore after his run. Charlotte was already up. He joined the others who were already seated on the roof terrace drinking freshly squeezed orange juice.

"Morning. How did you sleep?" he asked, kissing Charlotte.

"Oh, so-so," she replied.

"Well let's gets something to eat and then I'll head down to Soller to speak to the Inspector."

After breakfast James went into his study and looked through an old address book, searching for the telephone number of the CID office at his old station in Rotherhithe, London, which he then rang.

"CID Rotherhithe can I help you?" said a female voice.

"Could I speak to Bam Bam?" said James.

"Who's calling please?" asked the female.

"Just say it's a blast from the past," replied James.

"Detective sergeant Wiggins, can I help?" said a familiar voice.

"Bam Bam, you old dog! It's Semtex."

"I don't believe it! That is uncanny. I was talking about you just the other day to Sam Jones. How the hell are you?"

"I'm pretty good. So you're still there then."

"Well you know me. This is my manor and I'm not moving just to get promotion or to make room for some high-flying graduate who doesn't know his arse from his elbow. Anyway are you still in 'the job'?"

"No mate. I meant to send you a Christmas card over the years but you know, good intentions and all that. I left about eight years ago. I thought I'd go and make some decent money for a change and I went into business. I've just moved out to Mallorca."

"You jammy bugger! I always knew you'd do well. Bloody hell, Semtex! I can't believe it. So to what do I owe this honour?"

"Well believe it or not I need a favour. I'm trying to find out about a guy who moved to my village a few weeks ago from Bermondsey. All I know is he called himself Steve. He's an IC1, about mid-thirties, five feet ten, short dark hair, heavy build, with two front teeth missing either side of his incisors and a double scar on his cheek. Ring any bells?"

"That's Chas Daly. No doubt about it. You say that 'scrote' has moved to your village in Mallorca. That explains a lot. He wasn't a player in your day but he certainly is now. He's been inside for possession with intent to supply, did a five-year stretch for armed blagging and was a sidekick of Danny Kusemi until they fell out. You wouldn't know Danny. He came over from Peckham a few years ago and controls most of the drugs supply in south London. He's a vicious bastard and your mate Steve aka Chas was running with him until he did a runner with quite a tidy sum, so one of my touts tells me. Danny's put the word out and even put a bounty on his head, so Chas had better lie low or he'll be brown bread."

"He is lying low: about six feet under, or at least he will be. He was murdered two days ago. I found him in his house. He had been badly beaten."

"Shit! That's Danny's MO. He's been flagged and I'm supposed to be told by Special Branch if he leaves the country. Mind you he's probably on a ringer passport."

"What does this guy Danny look like?" asked James.

"He's about 40, stocky build, five feet eleven, and swarthy skin, with short, cropped dark hair. He's got a tattoo on his forearm, which reads 'The Turk', that's his nickname. He's a bit tasty with a blade too. Do you think you've seen him?"

"Maybe. I think he might be looking for me, or at least for something I have."

"Listen you be careful. If it is Danny who's out there he will cut you as soon as look at you, if he thinks you'll get in his way. We think he's responsible for at least three murders here over the past couple of years but I think he's got somebody at The Flying Squad in his pocket. The word is the money that Chas half-inched was Danny's payoff to the Russian mafia after he killed one of their dealers in a fight and he doesn't want to lose face. That's why it has to be Danny; 'cos he always does his killing himself and the guy you described has to be Chas Daly. He hasn't been seen around here for weeks and Daly and Danny went everywhere together with that mongrel of a dog that Daly called 'Lamps'–he was a big Chelsea fan. Look, what can I do to help? Do you want me to come over there and speak to the local plod?"

"You just want a holiday in the sun!" laughed James.

"Too right son!"

"Well look, give me your mobile number. I'm going to speak to the local police again today. I'll get them to liaise directly with you. They may want you to come and I.D. the body. Did he have any family?"

"Only some 'skaghead' of a sister who's on her last legs. She won't want to know. She's his only next-of-kin as far as I know. You know some heads are going to roll over this one."

"Why's that?" asked James.

"Well between you and me, Kusemi is supposed to be under surveillance. Somebody at The Yard is going to get their balls chopped off for this. But anyway that's another story. Listen me old mucker, you take care. Watch your back and hopefully I'll see you soon and we can have a couple of Sangrias or whatever they drink over there. Cheers."

James came off the phone with his mind reeling from the revelations of the conversation with his old friend. He had no doubt that Chas and Steve were one and the same. Bam Bam, or Reginald – which is why he preferred to be known by his nickname – had more local knowl-edge than any police officer James had ever met and he was never wrong. In hearing about this Danny Kusemi, James' worst fears had been realised. He went to tell Charlotte he was leaving for the police station, when there was a knock on his front door. He opened the antique wooden internal doors and saw his neighbour Brian who lived opposite him. James immediately unlocked the outer glazed front door.

"Good morning Brian, everything alright?" he asked.

"Well no, not really. I have a huge favour to ask."

James could see that the normally bubbly Brian was soft-spoken and obviously distressed.

"It's my mother," he continued. "My sister rang me about twenty minutes ago from England. My mother's had a heart attack and has been rushed to hospital. They don't think she's going to make it. I've just booked a flight and check-in closes in an hour and I can't get hold of Gemma. She's got the car and has forgotten to take her mobile and all the taxis are booked solid. I was wondering if…"

"Of course Brian," interrupted James, "I can take you. Just let me tell Charlotte and grab the car keys."

"I really appreciate it James. Could you ask Charlotte to keep an eye out for Gemma? I haven't had time to leave her a note or anything but I'll ring her later."

"Of course. Two seconds."

With that James informed Charlotte of what had happened and he and Brian set off for Palma Airport.

James got to the airport and parked outside the Departures terminal in the dropping off zone, but went in to make sure Brian made his flight in time. Satisfied that Brian was going to make it, he turned to make his way back to his car when to his right in the open expanse of the airport terminal he noticed several rows of silver coloured lockers. Most of them had their keys in them, which had a round green disc with their numbers on them. James' heart jumped into his mouth. He walked closer to them looking for evidence to confirm that this was what he had been looking for. He placed his hand in his pocket and pulled out the key he had found, fully intending to hand it in to the Inspector, but for his act of mercy towards his neighbour. The green disk was the same. It had the number 27 on it. He looked for this locker number 20, 21, 22, 23, 24, 25, 26, 27. There it was. His heart was now racing. His eyes now zoomed in on the lock. It had no key in it.

James furtively looked around him for some sign that he was being watched. He looked for any visible signs that the locker had been marked and he checked to see if there were any CCTV cameras covering the locker area. There were none apparent. He walked past the locker and sat down on a long plastic bench within view of his locker, to take stock of the situation. He had, quite by accident, due to his goodwill gesture to his neighbour, stumbled across a very important missing piece of the jigsaw. He had in his possession the key to a locker that someone was perhaps killed for. Someone who had by all accounts 'done a runner' with a substantial amount of money, albeit the proceeds of crime and there was a strong possibility that it may have been stashed in the locker only twenty-feet from where he now sat. Was it the thought of finding this crucial evidence to help solve a motive for the murder or was it the thought of a potentially large sum of money that was exciting him? Or both? James felt confused by his own feelings.

After a few minutes of deliberating his next move, he stood up with intent and walked directly to the locker. He inserted his key and turned it clockwise. He heard a click and the lock released and he slowly opened the door. Inside he saw a brown leather holdall. "Shit!" he said under his breath. He looked around, half expecting to see either Danny Kusemi or the stocky Inspector coming towards him, but neither did. James looked for the zip of the bag, which he located underneath. He had to turn the bag over, which he cursed as he did so but realised that the holdall was of significant weight. He cautiously unzipped the bag by about a foot, half expecting an alarm to go off or some other anti-theft device to activate. He peered inside, pushing down gently on one half of the bag to increase the gap. There it was looking back at him. What he had suspected was confirmed and in unzipping the bag still further it was confirmed again and again. The bag was full of money. Bundles and bundles of money. There were bundles of £50 Sterling notes, high denomination notes in US dollars and in Euros, and that was only the top row. He quickly zipped the bag back up and went to lock the locker again only to find that it required another 1 Euro coin to re-lock it. He frantically dived into his pockets with both hands looking for coins and to his relief, pulled one out of his pocket, inserted it and re-locked the locker, removed the key depositing it in his pocket as he quickly made for the relative safety of his car.

He got in and sat with his hands on the steering wheel. He looked straight ahead as if in a trance. The enormity of his discovery was beginning to hit home to him. He couldn't think straight. He had to get out of there. He turned the key in the ignition and drove off. He headed back through the tunnel and ended up outside the police station, as if some force had navigated his way for him, he was surprised to find himself there. He was clearly still in awe of his discovery. He sat in his car trying to work out in his head what he was going to tell the police. He was having a battle with his conscience. James could not help thinking what if he was to take the bag, after all where would the money go? It would probably be confiscated and returned to The Metropolitan Police or kept by the Spanish Police. It was certainly the proceeds of drug dealing and other similar crime but he couldn't help thinking how it might change his life and the lives of his family. James was by no means well-off but he had enough to get by and hopefully his new hotel would provide a decent living, but there was still risk involved. With that sort of money he wouldn't have to worry about money ever again. He estimated by the size of the bag that there could be anything up to £1 million or its equivalent. He tried to justify this possible action by telling himself that he would donate a significant chunk of it to charities with him imagining himself as some kind of philanthropist. He decided to go inside and for now apprise the Inspector of the information he had been given by his friend Bam Bam and to pass on his telephone number.

He went inside and requested to speak to Inspector Martinez. A short time later he appeared and ushered James into a small room.

"So what have you come to tell me?" he asked.

"As I told you I used to be a police officer, so I rang a friend of mine in the police in London. He has got a name for the man who was killed. He says his name was Chas, which is short for Charles and his surname was Daly. I have the detective's mobile phone number for you as well. He would like to speak to you. He says that this man was a well-known supplier of drugs and has served time in prison. It is believed that he came to Mallorca to get away from one of his criminal associates, as he had stolen some money from him. This man is called Danny Kusemi. My colleague will give you full details of this man. He believes Kusemi is probably responsible for the murder. He says that he has killed in the same way before and he had motive to do it. I'll write down my colleague's name and number," said James.

The Inspector produced a pen and a paper and James wrote down the details.

"By the way, we think he's entered the country on a false passport and he may have hired a silver coloured car, possibly a Volkswagen Passat. I was out running last night and I saw a man who matched this Kusemi's description acting suspiciously near Fornalutx. You will be able to get his photograph sent to you by my colleague. That's about it for now," said James.

"One question for you. Why do you think this Kusemi would still be in the area if he has done this?" asked the Inspector.

"I think he's looking for something, maybe the money that was taken from him," replied James.

"It is very risky for him to do this, no?"

"I agree but then I don't think this guy is frightened by much, if what my colleague says about him is anything to go by."

"Ok. I will ring this Detective Sergeant Wiggins," said the Inspector, looking down at what James had written.

"Thank-you for the information. I will see you out."

James left and returned to his car, feeling very guilty at not disclosing his knowledge of the money to the Inspector.

"What am I doing?" he said to himself as he sat in his car.

He returned home to find Charlotte and the boys were out. He paced up and down in his living room trying to work out what he should do. He knew what the right, sensible and law-abiding thing to do was, but temptation had been placed in his way. He was curious to see just how much money was in the bag. After about half an hour of pacing and deliberating James found himself heading back to his car.

He set off, not really knowing where he was going but before he knew it he was driving through the tunnel and was heading in the direction of Palma airport. He pulled into the airport and parked his car in the multi-storey car park. He was going to go and get the bag, if nothing else to recover it for the police, he told himself. However he decided, as a precaution, to try and disguise his appearance, in case of being captured on CCTV. He had a change of clothes in his boot from being at the beach earlier in the week and he changed into these, put on his sunglasses and put on a baseball cap. He also took a cloth he used to clean his windscreen, with the intention of cleaning any fingerprints he may have left on the locker from the previous visit. To all intents and purposes James was already halfway to committing a criminal offence by his actions. The 'actus reus' was about to take place but they would have to prove his 'mens rea'. He didn't know exactly what his intentions were himself at that stage but all he knew was that he wanted to collect that bag, count the money and after that he would decide his course of action.

He walked into the departure terminal for the second time that day, looking all around, trying not to look suspicious but feeling as if he was walking headlong into an abyss. He approached the locker, inserted the key and opened the locker door. The bag was still there. He lifted it out and set it on the ground. He furtively looked round and discretely wiped the locker all over with his cloth, picked the bag up and headed for the exit. A couple of uniformed Guardia Civil police officers were standing outside the exit. James froze and stopped in his tracks, his eyes fixed on them, looking for some indication that they were waiting for him. They appeared to be more interested in a passing blonde-haired woman than him, so he chanced it and continued walking out the exit and behind them. He walked on without looking back, waiting for them to shout at him to stop but he reached the entrance to the car park and looked back. They were still there chatting and looked relaxed and totally uninterested in him.

He continued until he reached his car, opened his boot and placed the bag in it, got in and drove off, trying to look as normal and inconspicuous as possible.

He continued driving towards Fornalutx, looking ahead for roadblocks and checking in his rear-view mirror constantly for fear of being followed. He entered his village and parked his car in the municipal car park. James wondered what to do with the bag. He got out of the car and went to the recycling bins at the front of the car park. The bins were full to overflowing and people had left large black bin bags full of recycling material beside them. He tipped the contents of one bag into another and walked back to his car and opened the boot. He placed the brown leather holdall inside the black bin bag and walked off carrying the now disguised bag over his shoulder. He walked up the steps of the plaça and into his street, walking past his house to the house next door that he was working on. He unlocked the heavy wooden door, went inside and setting the bag on the ground, locked the door behind him. He then carried it to a room at the back of the house, near to a window opening, where there was more light. No one could see him as the rear of the property was surrounded by high stone walls offering total privacy. He unzipped the bag and began to take out its contents and place them on the bin bag. He worked quickly and methodically and when all the bundles of notes had been removed, he counted them. There were 147 bundles. James counted the contents of several bundles and found each contained £5,000. Accounting for the fact that there were about twenty bundles of Euros and Dollars, he estimated that the total was about £735,000. He quickly put the bundles into the black bin bag, concerned that the brown leather bag might have been fitted with a tracking device. He lifted the bin bag and carried it up the stairs and placed it in a small wooden cupboard built into the wall in one of the bedrooms. He took the brown leather bag and examined it closely, unzipping the pockets and checking for any possible areas a tracker could have been hidden. It seemed to be devoid of anything of this kind. James still decided to move the bag to another place and took it outside and placed it between the outside wall of the house and a terrace and covered it with the large variegated leaves of the ivy that was growing up the wall. He then went back inside and out through the front door, locking it behind him. He walked the few steps to his front door and went inside. Charlotte was in the kitchen preparing the evening meal.

"Hi!" said James.

"Hi! Have you changed?" asked Charlotte, looking confused.

"Yeah, yeah. What are you making?" asked James, trying to change the subject.

"Risotto with garlic prawns. Did you go to the police station today?" she enquired.

"Yes I saw the Inspector and told him what Bam Bam told me on the phone."

"And the key, did you give him the key?"

James remained silent, looking sheepish.

"James did you give the Inspector the key or not?" demanded Charlotte.

"Not," replied James. "Look I can't keep this to myself any longer. Where are the boys?"

"Upstairs playing on the Wii."

"Right as you know I took Brian to the airport this morning and when I was coming back to the car you'll never guess what I saw."

"What? Just tell me," said Charlotte, clearly agitated at the fact that he hadn't handed in the key.

"I found the locker. You were right it was a locker key. I opened the locker and there was a holdall inside full of money. I came back here without it but you were out so I went back for it and I've got it next-door. There is over £735,000 in it!" said an animated James.

"I don't care if there's £10 million in it. You are playing with fire and you've got to give it to the police. You could end up getting arrested. What if they were to find it next door? You'd be in serious trouble. What on earth were you thinking?"

"Charlotte I don't know why I did it. It was the fact that I just stumbled over it like that and there it was at my disposal, without anyone the wiser. It was a moment of stupidity. I'm sorry." James approached Charlotte looking for a sign of her forgiveness, which he eventually got in the form of a half-hearted hug.

"Well tomorrow is the start of the fiesta here in the village and the place will be choc-a-block, so you had better get up early and hand it in."

"Ok I will. I tell you what, I'll ring the Inspector to see if I can see him tomorrow."

James took out his wallet and produced the card that Inspector Martinez had given him. He rang the number.

"Si."

"Hola. This is James Gordon from Fornalutx," said James.

"Oh yes, how are you?"

"I'm good. I was wondering if I could come to the police station tomorrow to see you?" enquired James.

"Well not tomorrow. I am going to Barcelona for three days but I will be back on Monday. Can it wait or is there something I can do for you now? I am at my home but…"

"No, no." interrupted James, "It will keep until Monday."

"By the way I spoke to your Detective Sergeant Wiggins. He is coming over to see me on Tuesday when I get back from Barcelona and I have circulated the photograph he sent me of the suspect Danny Kusemi. So now we wait. I have to go now but I will see you on Monday no?"

"See you Monday. Adios."

James felt that he had just had his sentence deferred. He would have to come clean about what he had done and hopefully he could make it out that it was his willingness to help that led to his lack of judgement regarding the money. A thought occurred to him of how would the police know how much should be in the bag? He may still find himself accused of stealing some of the money, without having taken any. He would have to return the bag and its contents to the locker and just hand over the key. He was to take Adam to his new school on the outskirts of Palma on Monday morning, so he could continue on to the airport and return it and then go to see Martinez as planned.

5

THE FIESTA

The next morning James awoke to find the tiled floor of the roof terrace was wet. It had obviously been raining during the night but the sky was a clear blue and it was going to be another beautiful day. Today was the start of the village fiesta, which went on for three days. He knew what to expect but had never actually been in the village during the fiesta but by all accounts the village became packed with Mallorcans from all over the island.

James strolled down to the village grocery store on the corner of the plaça and picked up a basket, filled it with some breakfast essentials of a fresh baguette, eggs, croissants, and milk before getting into the haphazard queue that resembled more of a scrum than a queue. Some of the indigenous population tended to hover about the till and catch the eye of the solitary cashier, in what was a busy store. This tended to cause some resentment amongst holiday-makers, especially those from Britain and Germany who did not agree with this form of favouritism. James had accepted this as part of Mallorcan life and did not let it annoy him, as it once would have. He returned home and carried the provisions up to the roof terrace where Charlotte was squeezing fresh oranges, which came from their neighbour Marta's orange grove.

"Oh good you got some milk," said Charlotte.

"What's happening this morning then?" asked James.

"Well it's the gift-giving ceremony for the elderly residents, as far as I know. Then they have the running of the bull in the afternoon."

"We must go to see both of those and get to the plaça early to get a good seat."

"I told Garth and Jenny we'd see them at Café sa Plaça and we can have some tapas while we're there."

After breakfast, James drove the short distance into Soller and parked the car. He walked past the colourful Plaça Constitucion, dominated by the enormous parish church of Sant Bartomeu. The church was built in a baroque style and the façade was designed by a pupil of Gaudi, Joan Rubi. As he walked, James stopped to give way to one of the antique trams, which ran to the Port de Soller and back. The orange and wooden trams were a reminder of bygone days having been built in 1913 but were still operational. He walked along Carrer de sa Lluna to C'an Martarino, the best butchers in the area for some meat and for their homemade sobrasada or sausages and then onto the delightful Finca Gourmet, the most comprehensive delicatessen for some bread, olives and cheese. James enjoyed the whole shopping experience in Soller. It was so laid back. For most of the time he didn't miss British supermarkets. If he needed anything that he couldn't get in Soller, there were plenty of supermarkets on the outskirts of Palma, most with British products for those expats who couldn't survive without HP sauce or Marmite.

Soller had lots of independent family run stores with traditional Mallorcan produce and some with shop-fronts that hadn't changed in a century. It was a charming town with a relaxed atmosphere. It had its fair share of sophistication in the form of The Grand Hotel of the five-star variety, to boutique hotels and award-winning pastry shops.

The town was a maze of narrow winding streets, full of eighteenth and nineteenth century fruit merchants', stone townhouses with green shutters, antique wooden doors and ornate grilles. It was a thriving town of about 12,000 inhabitants, many of whom, as in Fornalutx, where foreign residents, taken by this traditional Mallorcan town.

On returning to Fornalutx, James and his family made their way down the steps to the plaça below. It was now mid morning and already the plaça was a hub of activity. James spotted a waving hand and he saw Garth and Jenny already seated at a table and went to join them.

"Good morning! I see you've got us the best seats in the house," he said, as he and Charlotte joined them, while Adam and Reuben went to take a closer look at the temporary stage, which had been erected during the morning.

"How have you been? I don't think we've seen you since we heard about the English guy," said Jenny.

"I'm fine now. It wasn't the nicest thing in the world to find, but I'm over it now," replied James as he sat down.

"Have the police any suspects yet?" asked Garth.

"Yes as a matter of fact they have. It turns out our friend Steve was called Chas Daly and was linked to a major drug dealer from London. It seems he left in a hurry with money belonging to his boss and it appears he caught up with him. I have an old friend who is still in the police in London, he is coming over next week and this drug dealer, who is a bit of a nasty bugger, is the prime suspect, so I believe his description has been circulated, as being wanted in connection with the murder."

"It's certainly a nasty business, but I thought that guy was a bit strange," said Garth. "I know that Catalina said the police had taken his dog away so at least she's not going to be annoyed by him or his dog to be perfectly blunt. Mind you I think that house will take a while to shift when people realise it's been the scene of a murder!"

"Well anyway let's not dwell on that today. Today is a day for celebration. Can I get anyone a coffee?" asked Charlotte.

"We're fine," replied Jenny.

"I'll have a cappuccino," said James.

The plaça continued to fill and soon it was standing room only. The Mayor arrived and took his place on the stage and tested the PA system, as children began to gather at the base of the stage. Several bags full of gifts were carried onto the stage and everything was now ready. The proceedings started with an address by the Mayor in Catalan, welcoming everyone. Then came a conveyer belt like roll call of the names of the elderly village residents who, in turn climbed, or in the case of some, hobbled or were assisted onto the stage, in celebration of their achieving their respective ages of seventy or more. Each was handed a gift by a child and received a rapturous round of applause from the appreciative crowd. James sat enjoying the proceedings and soon it was Adam's turn to present a gift to their neighbour Marta, from whom he received an all-enveloping hug.

As the last of the gifts were presented, Adam and Reuben fought their way through the growing crowd and joined their parents at the table.

"I'm quite hungry. Can we get some tapas?" enquired Adam.

"Yes I think we'll order some for everyone," said Charlotte.

The afternoon was spent over a leisurely lunch and then some of the local young males began to gather at the bottom of the steps of the plaça. This marked the beginning of the 'running of the bull' in a similar display to the bigger version in Pamplona. A bull was to be released through the narrow cobbled streets while the testosterone – fuelled young men ran in front, trying to avoid being gorged by its horns. An area of the plaça was cordoned off and some council workers were on hand to stop any bystanders getting too close to the action. It proved to be a somewhat tamer affair than James had expected as the 'raging bull' was more akin to a 'slightly annoyed bullock' and the danger element seemed to be null and void but nonetheless, it was amusing to see the tradition being continued.

"Are you eating out tonight?" enquired Garth.

"Yes we're going to Café Med tonight as a treat for Adam before he starts his new school on Monday. He loves the chicken with tarragon there."

"Have you booked?"

"Oh yes. Everywhere will be packed tonight so we booked last week. What about yourselves?"

"We are eating at Es Turo tonight but we'll be down to the plaça early to get a seat for the music."

"We'll probably see you then. The boys love the music so we can't miss that. Anyway we're going back to the house for a while so we'll catch you later," said James.

The family made their way home and James checked the front door of his property next door, still feeling uneasy in the knowledge that he had deposited over £730,000 in cash in the house and had to return it to its former location on Monday, in an effort not to end up in a Spanish prison, if nothing else for his stupidity. It was still locked and secure but James wanted to physically check it, so as Charlotte and his sons went into their house, he motioned to Charlotte that he was going into the house next door.

He climbed the stairs and checked his hiding place. It was still there to his relief. He then went into the enclosed courtyard at the rear of the house and retrieved the brown leather holdall and found it to be slightly damp from the overnight rain, so he decided to bring it inside to dry it. It might be suspicious if the police were to find the bag and its contents back in the locker on Monday and the bag was obviously wet. Satisfied that his booty was still secure James locked up and returned home.

That evening they stepped out into their street to find it full of Mallorcan teenagers, none of who appeared to be from the village. As they approached the steps at the top of the plaça, James couldn't believe the sheer number of people below. They arrived at Café Med to be greeted by the owner Simon.

"Welcome, welcome, nice to see you. It's going to be a busy evening. Have you ever seen crowds like this before?"

"No! There must be nearly a thousand people all crammed into the square."

"Well there will be more to come and you know this goes on all night?"

"They certainly know how to enjoy themselves."

"Any word about you know what?" asked Simon in a quiet voice.

"Well the police are looking for someone who they believe is involved. He's probably done a runner back to the UK by now and he's a well known criminal, so I think it should be just a matter of time before he's caught," said James.

"Oh that's good news. The sooner that's put to bed the sooner we can all put it behind us. Now then what can I get you to drink?"

As they ordered, James noticed more and more people joining the melee. The crowds were now spilling out of the plaça and were now all along the street where their table was outside the restaurant. Just then Adam pointed into the crowd:

"Look! There's Nick!"

James turned round to see the familiar face of Nick, his wife Kirsty and their young daughter.

"I don't believe it!" shouted James in his best Victor Meldrew impersonation.

"I was wondering when we might bump into you. How are you all doing?" said Nick, shaking James by the hand and kissing Charlotte.

James reciprocated to Kirsty.

"We're pretty good, despite recent events," said James.

"Oh that sounds ominous," said Nick.

Nick and Kirsty were a couple James and Charlotte had met over the past three summers, when the couple, who now lived in London, holidayed in Fornalutx. Nick, who was a restauranteur, rented houses in the village over the summer, having come on summer holiday three years in succession. He was so captivated by it and by all it could offer for a family holiday, with good restaurants and good company, had returned year after year.

"It's a good one but best told over a drink or two. I'll get Simon to get a couple of extra chairs," said James.

As Simon provided chairs, the couple joined the family with their young daughter, who was trying in vain to sleep in her pushchair.

"Simon, can I have another bottle of the Macia Batle please and two more glasses?" asked James.

"Of course. Coming right up."

"When did you get here?" asked Charlotte.

"We arrived about an hour ago and it took us about twenty minutes to squeeze through all the people. It's a bit mad," said Kirsty in her Glaswegian brogue.

"It's the fiesta. Expect it to be like this until late morning tomorrow," said Charlotte.

"So what have you been up to?" asked Nick.

"You missed all the excitement. There was a murder just round the corner two days ago. It was a guy from London, who had just moved here. I met him for the first time the night before and called down to his house the next morning and I found him dead," said James.

"Bloody Hell!" said Nick and Kirsty in unison.

"You actually found him?" asked Kirsty visibly taken aback by the revelation.

"Yes. He wasn't in great shape," replied James.

"How had he been killed?" asked Nick.

"Well… if you really want to know… he had been beaten to death," whispered James not wishing Adam to hear.

Both of the new recipients of this further revelation screwed their respective faces up and Nick said, "Nasty. Anybody going down for it?"

"I've been helping the local Police. It turns out the guy was here using a false name and I think I've traced him as a drug dealer from Bermondsey, probably killed by his boss for making off with a very substantial wad of drug money, at least that's one line of enquiry," said James.

"Bloody Hell! Typical! The Great British scum. You just can't go anywhere. So he was a Bermondsey boy then was he? Interesting. So we come on holiday and we miss a gruesome murder and we nearly miss the fiesta. Never a dull moment here! Right that's it. I'm definitely moving here!" laughed Nick.

The bottle of wine was quickly finished and another one was ordered and the conversation continued for another hour until it was time for their young daughter to get to bed, as she was unable to sleep with all the excitement of the crowd around her. Nick and Kirsty said good-night with a view to catching up further the next day.

After paying for the meal, James and his family made their way towards Café sa Plaça slowly through the crowd. The live music was just starting but James was concerned at the sheer numbers in the crowd, so they walked up the wide steps which overlooked the plaça and the stage below and he lifted Reuben up onto his shoulders to get a better look at the musicians as they performed.

First up was the popular local band called Pa amb oli, which included two of Robert Graves' sons in the line up. Both of James' sons were evidently enjoying the spectacle but it soon became clear that Reuben was beginning to wilt. James took both the boys back and Charlotte put Reuben to bed. By that stage Adam was beginning to yawn and he decided to hit the hay also. Charlotte remained at the house while James decided to go back to the plaça to meet Garth and Jenny for a nightcap.

His street was still full to overflowing with people. He squeezed through and made his way down the crowded steps to the bottom. It was slow going and James was having second thoughts when through the crowd he saw a man standing on the bench beside the water fountain.

The man was about forty years old and appeared to be about six foot tall, although it was hard to tell as he was the only person standing on the bench, so he was head and shoulders above everyone else. He was of stocky build and had short, cropped hair. James stared at him from where he was. Could this be the same man who had passed him in the car whilst out running? Could this be Danny Kusemi? If it was, then why was he still here? The man was swigging from a bottle of beer and was looking around the crowd. He didn't appear to be with anyone else and he didn't seem interested in the band on stage. This fact alone worried James. The man hadn't spotted him, so he moved off away from the plaça, trying to keep the man in his line of sight. He managed to get through the crowd and made his way round behind the man and was now some fifty feet behind him. He could just make out the left hand side of the man's torso, the remainder of him being obscured by a large plane tree but the light on top of the fountain was illuminating him and James could clearly make out the little he could see of him. He felt sick with nerves. In his heart of hearts he felt that this was the man he had seen in the car. He was not good at remembering names but he never forgot a face. His mind raced trying to decide the best course of action. There really only was one: he had to ring the police. If he was wrong and this wasn't Kusemi, then the police would be slightly annoyed and so too would the man, but at least James would be able to sleep. If it was Kusemi then he would have brought a murderer into police custody and then he would definitely be able to sleep. It was a no brainer.

He moved further back away from the man but in line with him, to keep him in his view. James was aware that by now the features of the man were becoming blurred, as he hadn't brought his glasses with him. He took out his mobile phone and dialled the number for Inspector Martinez. He put a finger in his ear as the music was still deafening from where he was standing. He could hear a ringing tone.

"Si," said the recognisable voice of Martinez.

"Oh good you're there," said James, moving to one side momentarily to allow some people past.

"It's James Gordon and I'm in the plaça in Fornalutx," he started but stopped short.

In the instant he had looked away to let some people pass by, the man was no longer to be seen. James shuffled to one side to see if he had simply moved along the bench but no. He must be in the crowd, he thought. Could he be walking towards him? He had to find him. By now the music was even louder as he moved closer to where the man had been a few moments before. Any further conversation with the Inspector from his location was futile.

"I'll ring you back!" shouted James into his phone before hanging up.

He had to concentrate on finding the man and quickly without being compromised, or else the game was up. He moved slowly through the crowd, scanning all around him. He was conscious that if Kusemi had seen him, the opportunity for him to be stabbed was acute and he had to be alert. James was having to push past people quite forcibly, much to the annoyance of some, so he quickly followed it up with a constant "Perdon, perdon," not knowing if this in fact was Spanish for excuse me. Anyway, his problem was too big to worry about the aggrieved feelings of a few slightly drunk revellers. Panic began to set in. There was no sign of him. Could he have left? Could he have gone to the toilet? The closest toilets were at Café sa Plaça, so he pushed his way towards it. Outside he saw Garth and Jenny and went towards them, peering inside the crowded bar for any sign of the man.

"Ah you made it! We were beginning to think you weren't coming," said Garth standing up to retrieve a chair he had obviously been keeping for James.

"Listen I can't stay. Have you seen a man in the last five minutes or so go into Café sa Plaça wearing jeans and a red T-shirt? He is well-built, with a shaved head. It's important," said James, continuing to look around him.

"No. Lots of people have been coming and going. Can I help?" asked Garth, looking concerned.

"Garth, would you go into the bar and see if there is a man who fits that description inside and check the loos too and come and tell me?"

"Sure!" he said, as he quickly descended into the throng of people within the bar waiting to be served.

"Is everything OK James?" asked Jenny timidly.

"I don't know Jenny. I thought I saw a man who might be involved in the murder and I just want to make sure. It's unlikely that he would be here but I need to check," said James trying not to startle Jenny with the revelation that a murderer could be at large in their midst and that he had just sent her husband off to try and find him.

"Have you told the police?" she asked.

"I was on the phone to them a couple of minutes ago but then I lost sight of the guy and anyway it's so hard to hear yourself think in this place let alone speak on the phone."

"It's just I noticed that the two village police officers are on duty here tonight. If they're not around the square they are usually at Paco's bar… just if you need them," she added.

Garth returned to the table shaking his head.

"No sign in there. I checked both the men's and the ladies' toilets. There's no one even close to that description. Who is it that you're looking for? Is it someone connected to the murder?"

"Yes. I think he's here. I think it's the same guy I saw when I was out running. I'm not one hundred percent sure but I think it could be the man responsible for the murder."

"Why would he still be here?" asked Garth.

"I think he might be looking for me. It's a long story, suffice to say I need to find him before he sees me," said James.

"Look, I'll help you but it's like looking for a needle in a haystack and even then if you do find him, what are you going to do?" asked Garth.

"Garth I appreciate the offer but there is no point in getting you involved. I'm just going to have a quick look in the car parks and then go to bed. Don't worry and thanks anyway."

Garth shook his head and sat down.

"You be bloody careful!" he shouted after James, as James made his way through the crowd towards the car parks on the road leading out of the village on the northern side.

By the time he had reached the first car park the crowds had been mostly left behind save for a few people walking up and down the road. The first car park was full of cars. James thought he would look for a silver Volkswagen Passat car and if he found it he would call Inspector Martinez again and ask him to get the local police to watch it. He entered the car park, checking each car. There were plenty of silver cars but no VW Passats, like the one he had seen on his run. His problem would be if he found more than one, he thought, as he continued to the next car park.

He walked up and down the rows of parked cars in the second car park but there was no sign here either. All the way up the road cars were parked on either side and all the way round the bend leading out of the village. This would take forever, he thought but he felt he had to check. James continued up the road, checking cars as he went, until he was about half a mile out of the village in an area without streetlights. He began to feel vulnerable so he decided to call it a night and make his way back to the relative safety of his house. He wanted to check on his family so he rang home.

"Hello." answered Charlotte.

"It's only me. Everything alright?" he asked, trying to sound calm.

"Fine. It's pretty noisy though. I can hear the music quite clearly from the house. I'm just going to bed. Are you going to be long?" she asked.

"No. I'm coming home now. I'll be up in ten minutes. See you shortly."

James was somewhat relieved by the news so he set off for his house, back down the road heading for the plaça. As he walked down the road, several groups of people were walking up the road; some still drinking and others were clearly the worse for wear. In the distance, by the bakery, just as the road began to turn, he could make out the figure of a solitary person standing alone. The street was not well lit at that point and he could not make out whether it was a man or a woman. He couldn't take any chances but there was nowhere else to go. He was tired and he did not feel like walking the mile and a half round the village to come in by the only other direction. He walked on slowly, waiting for some teenagers who he could hear behind him, allowing them to catch him up. He slotted in behind them, using them as cover. He was now able to get a better look at the person and could now tell it was not the man he had seen earlier. He was even more relieved to find the two local police officers were now at the back of the plaça keeping a closer eye on the behaviour of some of the revellers.

James skirted the plaça and walked down the road with the intention of entering his street on the western side, away from the crowds. There were still large numbers of people milling around but he could move freely. As he approached a very busy Café Med, Simon, the owner, who was topping up the wine glass of a customer eating al fresco, spotted him.

"Ah James. Hang on and I'll return your gear to you," said Simon, heading into the restaurant and reappearing moments later armed with items of police regalia.

Simon had been hosting a Murder Mystery Dinner at his restaurant the previous evening and had asked James if he could borrow anything he might have to transform himself into his chosen character for the evening, namely a policeman. So Simon returned a pair of police issue handcuffs, epaulettes, a police whistle and chain and a police issue forage cap.

James bade Simon goodnight after stowing the items about his person, whilst keeping his forage cap in his hand, as he turned the corner, one street from his house, he stopped dead in his tracks and stared. Staring back at him from about twenty feet away was the man whom he had seen earlier. He had stopped too and both men stood and looked intently at one another, frozen to the spot. The man's reaction confirmed to James that this was Kusemi. Other people continued to walk between the two men, still static like two gunslingers in a spaghetti western. The words 'fight or flight' came into James' head and he weighed up his options. He could run back and alert the two police officers, but by the time he did that Kusemi would be long gone. He could take him on right there but Kusemi was a big man and would definitely be armed with at least a knife. James could handle himself but that could be suicide. It was Kusemi who broke the silence first.

"You have something that belongs to me and I want it back," he said, staring at James.

"If you are talking about the key you killed Chas Daly for, the police have it now. I know who you are, Kusemi. The police know who you are. There are twenty plain clothes and uniform police in the village looking for you right now. All I have to do is shout and you're nicked. The game is up; you've nowhere left to run and I'm here to arrest you for the murder of Charles Daly," started James.

"Bollocks! I know who you are too. It's amazing the information that money can buy. You're not 'Old Bill' any more and anyway you can't arrest me out here, you ain't got no authority. I know you ain't handed no key in to the police here. Fact. I ain't a fuckin' Muppet so if you know what's good for you, give me the fuckin' key!"

Kusemi was beginning to get agitated and as he spoke James saw him place his right hand round the back of his jeans.

"Leave the knife where it is!" shouted James, "I'm here to arrest you. Why would I have this?" asked James, putting on his police hat and producing his secreted handcuffs and holding them aloft for Kusemi to see.

"Listen, I'm telling you other police are here and I did give them the key. It was in a cigarette packet that

Chas obviously told you about but you killed him anyway. Oh and by the way, a friend of yours is here and he really wants to see you: Bam Bam," said James.

"That fat bastard! I'm not scared of him, or you. I want my fuckin' money and I ain't leaving until I get it. Look, there's enough for everyone. You give me the money and I'll split it with you, fifty-fifty. I know you have it or at least you have the key 'cos you ain't given it in. Fact", said Kusemi edging closer.

Just at that point James heard some voices speaking English from behind Kusemi and a group of men came round the corner. Before Kusemi had a chance to turn around, James seized the initiative and shouted:

"Quick Bam Bam he's here!"

Without checking to see if DS Wiggins from Rotherhithe CID was in fact behind him with other police, Kusemi bolted past James, making his way at speed down the road in the direction of Soller. James continued the pretence by running after him, half-heartedly, shouting as if to give an update to following police, before allowing Kusemi to make his retreat. He had even momentarily contemplated retrieving his ceremonial police whistle and blowing it but quickly ignored the urge to do so in what would have been akin to a scene from the *'Keystone Cops.'*

James turned and quickly ran back to his house and went inside. He locked his front door and closed the heavy internal wooden doors and locked them too. He sat down in an effort to catch his breath. He pulled out his phone to call Martinez but he couldn't get a signal, so he climbed the stairs and rang him from the house phone.

"Si, Martinez."

"Martinez, it's James Gordon again. I've just spoken to Danny Kusemi. He has just run off from me. He was on foot heading towards Soller from Fornalutx along the road that skirts the torrent, although he may have left his hire car down there. Can you get your guys to look for him?" said James spilling out the information as quickly as possible.

"Yes I will ring the station straight away. Did you speak to him?" asked Martinez.

"Yes I told him the police were looking for him and that I was there to arrest him. I think he has been buying some information from one of your officers though."

"That is a very serious thing to say. Why do you say this?" asked Martinez.

"Listen, I haven't told you everything. I have discovered a locker key. It was hidden in the cigarette packet Daly gave me. I think it's for a locker that contains Kusemi's money. I was going to give it to you when I see you on Monday. He asked me for it tonight and I told him that I had given it to the police. He said he knew I hadn't, stating it was amazing the information that money could buy. Either he was bluffing or else someone in your department is bent, you know is accepting money," said James.

"Yes, yes I know what it means," said a disgruntled Martinez. "Let me think about that, but in the meantime I will call the local police to search for him. That is all I can do as I am in Barcelona. I cannot get back any earlier, my wife would kill me. The truth is, it is our tenth wedding anniversary and we are here to spend time with her family. So, I will see you on Monday and I will let you know if they catch Kusemi. Adios."

Street scene Biniaraix

Antique tram Port de Soller

Fornalutx placa and church

Orange and lemon grove towards Biniaraix

Placa Constitucion, Soller

Binibassi

Port de Soller

Fornalutx

6

IT COULD HAVE
BEEN SAN JUAN

It had just been another quiet morning at the Serious Crime Department at Police HQ in Palma for Inspector Ramon Martinez of La Policia Nacional and he had been booking flights to Barcelona for his tenth wedding anniversary to spend a few days with his in-laws there, when the phone rang. Martinez answered and was informed that the Chief of Police in Soller had attended the scene of a murder in Fornalutx and he was to attend the scene. The details were vague but it appeared that a man believed to be a non-resident had been killed in a townhouse in the village and local police were speaking to an Englishman at the scene. Suddenly his thoughts of what to have for lunch evaporated and he set about getting his belongings to make his way to Soller to meet up with the Police there before going to the murder scene. Martinez had been a detective for nearly fifteen years and had experience of murder enquiries, but this was the first time he ever had to attend Fornalutx for something of this magnitude.

He lived some fifteen kilometres from the village, but he had a close friend who lived just outside the village and he would occasionally frequent a local bar there with his friend. To him it was a beautiful village somewhat spoilt by the sheer number of foreign owners, but as his friend, a builder, kept telling him, without the foreigners he would not have such a successful building firm. He also pointed out that Martinez himself could be viewed as a foreigner. His family had originally come from the Soller valley in Mallorca but his grandfather had emigrated to Puerto Rico at a time when many Sollerics went to San Juan, the capital of Puerto Rico or to France for work. It was only after Martinez and his younger sister had been born that his parents decided to move back to Mallorca, so although he felt Mallorcan, sometimes he felt that some Mallorcans treated him as a second class citizen.

He arrived at the Police station in Soller and went into the Chief's office to wait for him, having been told he was on his way back to the station with someone he wanted Martinez to interview. He made a cup of coffee and sat looking out of the first floor open window to the street below. He knew the Chief from Soller well, as they were both avid fans of Real Mallorca and football in general and they even used to play for a local Police team when they both worked in Andratx in the south west of Mallorca.

The Chief arrived and entered his office;

"Bon dia Ramon. Com va?" he enquired.

"Not bad. So what's the score here?" asked Martinez in Catalan.

"It's a bad one. It appears that a foreign guy in his mid-thirties had moved into a house in Fornalutx, near the bank and another English guy found him this morning in the house."

"Cause of death?" asked Martinez.

"We are not sure of exactly the cause of death, other than he received numerous heavy blows to the face and body. The house is a mess, it could be that someone was trying to rob him. There is no sign of forced entry to the house and apparently, from initial enquiries, the deceased lived alone. The body looks as if he took quite a beating before he was killed."

"Do you think this is sexually motivated? Is there anything to suggest the deceased was a homosexual?" asked Martinez.

"Why do you ask?" said the Chief.

"Well do you remember the murder a couple of years ago in C'an Picafort?"

"Well just what I read in the police bulletins and in the papers."

"That was a similar type, where it turned out the German guy had been seeing someone other than his long-term live-in lover, who came back early from work one day to find them in bed together. I just wondered if there were any similarities."

"I don't know. I suppose we'll have to wait for the post mortem. Anyway the guy who found him is downstairs."

"What do you think about him?" asked Martinez.

"Well I was hoping you would tell me. You are the expert after all," said the Chief smiling. "Personally I don't think he's our man. He lives in the village and says he was a policeman."

"Ok let's speak to him."

Martinez and the Chief then went down to the interview room where James was waiting for them.

Martinez was trying to size him up, but quickly got the impression that he was not responsible for the murder and despite requesting that James hand in his passport, which he refused to do, he released him asking him to contact Martinez if he wished to leave the island.

"Well what do you think?" asked the Chief when James had left.

"He's not our man. I would like to go to the scene now. Have arrangements been made for the body to go to the mortuary?" asked Martinez.

"Yes it will be taken once you have been to the scene. I have several officers there at the minute speaking to residents and preserving the scene. I have asked HQ to send over a Forensic Officer and he's on his way there as we speak. Here's the address," said the Chief handing a piece of paper to Martinez. "You can use the office next to mine when you return and let me know if you need any other resources."

"No problem, I'll see you later."

Martinez left and made his way directly to Fornalutx, ringing his wife on the way to inform her of what had happened and to say he would not be home at his usual time.

On arrival in the village he went towards the house. Local police, who were at both ends of the street, had cordoned off the street. He went to the front door and put on a pair of disposable gloves, not wishing to contaminate the scene. He also put on a forensic suit. Martinez hated wearing these as it made him sweat profusely but he was a consummate professional and he knew how important it was to preserve the quality of any potential forensic evidence. He also placed a mask over his mouth to prevent any contamination. Anyway it was good practice, he thought, as the local police officers looked on somewhat bemused by his attire.

He entered the entrada of the house and immediately noted the bloody paw prints on the tiled floor. He proceeded into the rear room where he had been told he would find the body. He saw the body of the murder victim lying on his side between two sofas. There was a large pool of blood around the victim's head and numerous sets of paw prints leading to and away from the body, which he had expected, having been told of the victim's dog. There were blood splashes on the sofas and on a broken lamp on the floor. He knelt down beside the body for a closer look. The victim had clearly been beaten around the face, as there was severe swelling around the eyes.

It was as violent a murder as Martinez had come across. Although he felt sickened by what he found he still had a steely determination to do his job in an efficient and methodical manner. Any mistakes would lead to him being severely reprimanded by his superior, who had been a detective for over thirty years and prided himself on a high clearance rate in gaining convictions for serious crime throughout Mallorca, a clearance rate which was much higher than on the Spanish mainland and in no small way was down to the professionalism of Martinez.

He continued to assess the scene and noted that there was indeed no sign of forced entry to the house, indicating that the killer had either entered through an unlocked door or perhaps the victim knew his killer and had invited him in. He checked the other rooms of the house and found that these were in a similar state to the living room, although there was no sign of blood in these rooms. It appeared that the killer might have been looking for valuables, as all the drawers had been pulled out and their contents strewn on the floor. He noted that the house only had one door, no garden but had a small roof terrace which was not overlooked but had no easy access to it except from across the steep pitched roof of the adjoining house but he quickly ruled this out as a point of entry as he noted there were no cracked tiles on the roof, which invariably there would be if a man walked or crawled across a terracotta tiled roof of this nature. A voice called from the entrada and Martinez went down to find a similarly suited forensic officer awaiting direction to the scene.

After a further hour of detailing the scene and the taking of swabs and samples by the forensic officer, Martinez arranged for the removal of the body to the mortuary in Palma. He spoke to the local officers outside and realised that a barman from a local bar had stated that the victim had been drinking in the plaça the previous night and police took his details. Martinez observed that a local television crew had set up at one end of the street and he told the local police to hold the scene until he contacted them later.

He took off his forensic suit and gloves and made his way back to his car and drove the short distance back to the police station in Soller. He washed up and went to report his findings to the Chief, who was waiting expectantly for him, after which he retired to the unfamiliar surroundings of his new temporary office, which would be his base for the next couple of weeks.

The Chief came in to see him before he left for the day and to make sure he did a press report on the murder, as it had now become apparent that the local press were aware of the incident and with that, he bade Martinez good luck and left, leaving him alone in a pensive mood, trying to think of anything he may have missed at the scene. He believed the victim to be English and that he was known as Steve. There had been no letters in the house nor any bank cards or anything on the victim to identify him, so there would be the task of fingerprinting the deceased at the mortuary. Martinez filed his report and because there was no more he could do and as it was going to be a busy day the next day, he released the officers from the scene by phone and made his way home.

It was nearly ten o'clock before he reached his house in Palmanyola, an urbanisation outside of Palma on the way to Soller. Martinez had lived there for ten years with his wife Maria and his two young sons. He had met his wife whilst on a police training course in Barcelona over eleven years previously and had visited her every month for a year before they got married and she moved to live with him in Mallorca from her native Barcelona. He had planned to take his wife and family to see her relatives that weekend to coincide with their tenth wedding anniversary so he would have a lot of work to do in order to be allowed the leave of absence that had already been approved. The murder investigation would take priority with his boss but his wife had not seen her parents for some months, so he hoped that he could still take her.

His wife was in the living room watching television when he arrived home.

"I have cooked you some lamb, you must be hungry. It's been a long day for you," she said, giving Ramon a hug.

"Yes it has been a long day," he agreed slumping onto a sofa. "How has your day been?" he asked.

"Fine. I went to the market this morning and Maria Catal called this afternoon with her boys, so our boys have only just gone to bed, if you want to look in on them."

"Yes I will."

Martinez went to his son's room and looked in. His twin boys were eight years old and shared a bedroom and on hearing the door open both boys lifted their heads.

"Papi!" they cried in unison.

Ramon went over to each boy in turn and kissed them goodnight before returning to the kitchen where his wife had set out his late supper.

"Ah that smells good," he said, sitting down at the table.

He began eating while Maria joined him after pouring them both a glass of local red wine.

"Listen, I wasn't going to tell you until tomorrow but I've booked us flights to Barcelona tomorrow night. I've spoken to your father and everything is arranged. It was going to be a surprise, but in light of what's happened I thought it best to tell you."

"Oh that's so sweet of you Ramon. Will we still be able to go?" asked Maria.

"It should be fine. I've already had my leave approved so it just means I'm going to be very busy tomorrow."

"Well, I will make you some food to take with you for tomorrow."

After his meal both Maria and Ramon retired to bed.

It was an early start the next morning and Ramon was up and out of the house by 6am. He spent all the morning at the mortuary fingerprinting and then attending the post mortem. He liaised with the local police in Fornalutx and later that day received a phone call from James informing him of the true identity of the deceased and of the name of a suspect called Danny Kusemi. He told Ramon of a potential motive for the murder and gave him the phone number of a detective in London who may be able to help. Ramon decided to ring the contact straight away.

"Rotherhithe CID can I help you?" said a female voice.

"Hello this is Inspector Martinez from The National Police in Mallorca. Could I speak to Detective Sergeant Wiggins?"

"DS Wiggins. Can I help?"

"Hello my name is Ramon Martinez and I am the investigating officer in a murder enquiry in Mallorca. I have been given your name by a James Gordon, who I believe was a former colleague of yours."

"Yes that's right, he told me to expect your call."

"We have a victim of a murder who we believe might be someone who you knew. He was about 35 years old, short dark hair and had two prominent scars on his left cheek…"

"Did the body have a tattoo on the left shoulder of a heart with MUM written in it?" interrupted Wiggins.

"Yes it did," replied Ramon.

"Then unless I'm very much mistaken, you have the lifeless body of one Charles Anthony Daly but if you can send me a set of his fingerprints, I can have that confirmed officially."

"Did you know this man and also this Danny Kusemi who I believe you think may be responsible?"

"Unfortunately Ramon, I knew this pair all too well. We crossed paths more times than I care to remember. They both worked closely together and have a string of convictions ranging from serious assault, to robbery and both were big players in the importation and distribution of cocaine, heroin and anything else you can think of. Daly was Kusemi's most trusted runner; his right hand man, that is until Daly did a runner, I mean ran off with what is believed to be a substantial amount of money belonging to Kusemi.

"Kusemi put a bounty on his head, that is, he would pay a reward to someone who found him but his instructions were that no-one was to kill Daly. He wanted that pleasure for himself. We believe Kusemi is responsible for at least two murders in London, we've never had sufficient evidence to charge him but it sounds like Danny's work alright. I've already taken the liberty of putting out an All Ports alert for him at the ports and airports but I believe he is travelling on a false passport, just as Daly would have been. Listen, I can come over to help in the investigation if you like. I just need you to send a fax to my boss requesting my attendance. The other thing is Daly's only next of kin is a drug addict sister who will not want to identify him. I will be able to do that and I'm sure we could have a beer or two after."

"Well actually I think it would be good to have you assist us, especially if this Kusemi might still be on the island. I will send through a formal request for you to attend to identify the body. I will be away for a few days, but will be back on Monday."

"Not a problem, look forward to working with you. I'll sort out my flights for say Monday or Tuesday. I'll ring you before I book them to make sure everything is still on. Bye for now."

"See you next week. Oh before you go I will need you to send me an up to date photo of this Kusemi so I can release it to Police around the island and at the airport."

"No problem I'll have that e-mailed to you in the next half hour."

Martinez spent the remainder of the day on press releases and updating his boss on the developments in the case, regarding the suspect and the involvement of UK Police. His leave was still approved, the police on the island were now on alert for anyone fitting the description of Kusemi and his photo had been circulated.

There was nothing further he could do that day and anyway he had the more pressing task of driving into Palma and picking a wedding anniversary present for his wife before he returned home to pack for their long weekend trip to Barcelona.

He drove into the city just as the rush hour traffic was beginning to form. He didn't have long to park, choose something and get home. Some of the shops in Palma closed from early afternoon, a hang over from the days when everyone took a siesta. However most of the larger stores and those in the shopping centres tended to stay open right throughout the day so he would still have sufficient choice.

As he set off he had no idea what to buy his wife or exactly where to go. Most of the main shops were concentrated along Passeig des Born and towards Plaça Major, where there were upmarket clothes and shoe shops. However he knew his wife liked the locally produced high-class Mallorcan artificial pearls.

He parked the car and made his way to Plaça Rosari where he knew there was a shop specialising in these.

It was a busy Friday afternoon and people were leaving work or sitting outside the numerous street cafés. Commuter traffic mingled with tourists in their hire cars out sight-seeing, interspersed with a sprinkling of open-topped guided tour buses and the old traditional horse-, drawn carriages; still popular with tourists getting a closer view of the city.

Ramon entered the store and asked to see some necklaces within his price range and eventually picked one he felt his wife would like and had it gift-wrapped. Happy with his choice, he made his way back to his car and drove the short distance to his home on the road between Palma and Soller.

He returned home to find his wife and boys in the kitchen. He covertly slipped into his bedroom and put his gift in his suitcase before returning to the kitchen.

"Papi you're home!" exclaimed his sons, running up to give their father a welcoming hug.

"Hey. How are you all today? Are you looking forward to seeing your grandfather tonight?" he enquired.

"Yes we are. I hope Grandfather Mayol has some sweets for us."

"Oh I'm sure you will be spoilt rotten," said Ramon. "Have you got your suitcase ready?" he asked, kissing his wife.

"I've been ready for hours. So have the boys. We're all looking forward to it. Well, how was your day? You look tired," said Maria stroking his face.

"I'm OK. I got done what I needed to do, so now is our time. I'm just going to throw a few clothes into my

UNDER A MALLORCAN SKY

bag and I'll be ready in a few minutes," he said, heading for his bedroom.

The flight to Barcelona that night was uneventful and arrived in just in time to drop the boys off with their Grandfather, while Ramon and Maria headed to their favourite restaurant close to The Ramblas area of the city, for a a romantic candle-lit dinner to celebrate their tenth wedding anniversary. He could now relax, at least for 48 hours.

7

GIVE US THIS DAY OUR 'DALY' BREAD

A vibration came from Kusemi's front jeans pocket and he pulled out both mobile phones to find a text message from an associate called 'Kingpin'. The message read: 'Urgent – C U at Blue in 10'. This meant that he was to make his way, in heavy traffic, along Rotherhithe New Road to meet Kingpin in a pub they both frequented.

Kusemi made his way along Lower Road and turned into Southwark Park Road, trying to think what the urgency for the meeting was. Kingpin was involved in some of Kusemi's larger drug deals. In fact, after Chas Daly, he was his most important 'runner'. He parked his car and walked the few hundred yards towards the Lord Admiral public house. He walked in and Kingpin was already seated with drinks on the table.

"What's so fuckin' urgent then?" said Kusemi, sitting down at the table.

The bar was empty except for old Dave, the bar fly and an elderly couple of pensioners sipping half pints of ale in a corner.

"You ain't gonna like this. You ain't gonna fuckin' believe this."

"Spit it out!" shouted Kusemi, not known for his patience.

"Daly's fucked off with the money from last night," said Kingpin in a matter of fact way.

"Bollocks. I spoke to him with you last night and he's stashed the cash and I'm seein' him in about an hour," said Kusemi aggressively, eyes bulging as he spoke.

"Look all I know is that Irish Mickey saw Daly leave his flat at about six this morning and he was carrying two suitcases, he drove off and he hasn't come back to the flat yet. I just tried to ring him and his phones off."

"I'll ring him now. You've got it all wrong. Chas might be fuckin' stupid but he ain't that fuckin' stupid."

Kusemi pressed his speed-dial button and dialled Chas' mobile. His phone was switched off.

"Right well his phone's off, I'll give you that, which is a bit fuckin' strange."

Kusemi then rang Daly's back up mobile. This was also switched off. This had never happened before. Even when Daly got arrested he always rang Kusemi no matter what.

"He's either been nicked or even worse, the fuckin' Russians have got him. Either way, I'm not fuckin' impressed. He's running around with a serious fuckin' bundle from last night and I've got to have it sorted by in a couple of weeks to give to Boris or I'm fucked, so leave the drinks and let's get round to Daly's flat."

Both men drove round to the flat in a new part of Docklands that had seen regeneration on a large scale, with numerous new housing developments overlooking the River Thames. Daly had chosen his second floor flat as there was only one way in and it was not overlooked, giving the Police limited ability to ever conduct a drugs raid. Daly often joked he could always swim for it if he had to. Kusemi kept a key to Daly's flat so gaining entry was not a problem. In the mood he was in, gaining entry without a key would not have posed much of a problem to him, as he would have forced entry without hesitation.

Once inside both men looked for signs of anything that would confirm or deny their fears. These fears were now beginning to play on Kusemi's mind. Chas had always been a loyal foot soldier and he had done well financially, but Kusemi now for the first time began to doubt his loyalty. The loyalty had been built over a number of years, through a perverse admiration of Kusemi by Daly, but in truth Kusemi knew that a great part of his loyalty was based on fear of Kusemi. Had Daly finally had the bottle to try and make a life for himself with a life-changing amount of Kusemi's money? It was beginning to look like it.

Kusemi and his associate began to open drawers and wardrobes for any sign of Daly having taken clothes and other essentials for an 'extended vacation'. Daly's dog was also gone and its food and water bowls where nowhere to be seen. His wardrobe was only half-full. A favourite leather jacket and all his designer watches were absent. This fact alone in an instant seemed to confirm Kusemi's fears.

"He's a fuckin' dead man!" he shouted, as he punched a stud wall so hard that his fist went through it, leaving a fist-size hole.

He turned to Kingpin, his face red with rage. His chest was visibly moving in and out as he spat out his instructions.

"Get the word out Daly's on the run. Whoever gets him is in line for ten grand... no fuckin' twenty grand. They can give him a right good spankin' but I want to finish him. Got that?" he demanded.

"Yeah. Sorted," said Kingpin.

"Well fuckin' get on with it then!" he bellowed, as Kingpin turned quickly on his heels and made a sharp exit, leaving Kusemi alone in Daly's flat, mulling over how he could have been so stupid as to let Daly have access to such a large amount of cash. This was soon replaced by a sharp pain and a quickening of his heart at the realisation that if he did not have the full amount of money to pay to the Russian mafia in three weeks HE was a dead man.

One morning a fortnight later, Kusemi's mobile rang. The number was withheld.

"Yeah?" he answered cautiously.

"Sam it's me," came a recognisable voice. Kusemi was speaking to his SCD7 Police handler from The Flying Squad and his codename was Sam. Unbeknown to his fellow criminals, Kusemi was a Metropolitan Police Flying Squad paid informant. As such, he was not supposed to be involved directly in crime other than in supporting roles such as being a driver. This fact was being completely disregarded and in fact his handler was being paid handsomely by Kusemi.

"Well what have you got for me?" he asked.

"I need to see you in the usual place in half an hour and bring a large one."

"Ok. See you there."

Kusemi recovered three bundles of bank notes each containing £5,000 from a hiding place in a sofa in his living room and placed them into separate brown envelopes and put them into his inside coat pocket. He believed his handler had knowledge on the whereabouts of Daly, so he would expect a reward. He would offer him five grand but may have to give more for this sort of information. He set off to rendezvous with his handler in a pub car park on the north of the River Thames and drove in and parked his car. He spotted a vehicle with his handler and he got in.

"I hope you've got what I want?" he said.

"I have got more than you could fuckin' have ever dreamt of," said his handler, who Kusemi had had on his payroll for some years.

"Well what's it gonna cost me this time? You know he fuckin' cleaned me out," said Kusemi.

"The word is that you were giving twenty grand for his whereabouts. I can give him to you on a fuckin' plate. I can give you country, town, house number and what he fuckin' had for breakfast if you want. So the question is, is that worth twenty large to you?"

"Sharkey, I'm skint! I've got fifteen on me and I'll get you the other five. You know I'm good for it. So cut the shit, here's fifteen," said Kusemi, reaching into his pocket and producing the three brown envelopes, which his handler took and placed in his pocket.

"You have no idea the palms I've had to grease over this one. Your man is no fuckin' fool though. He covered his tracks pretty well but not well enough. Guess where he holed up?" said Sharkey with a grin.

"I haven't time to fuckin' guess. Just fuckin' tell me where he is, 'cos I can't wait to see the look on his fuckin' stupid little face as I do him," said an agitated Kusemi.

"Alright, alright keep your hair on. He's in Majorca. I have a contact there and he has traced him to some little village in the mountains. I've got it written down for you. Here it is. He is staying in a house on this street and this is the number. Don't ask me how but it's kosher."

"The cheeky bastard! He thought he could get away with this and head for the sun. To be honest, I thought he would have gone down the Costas but I think he knows I have too many of the crew down there," said Kusemi with a wry smile.

"Whatever comes next I don't want to know but for fuck sake make sure you get there covert, otherwise you'll be flagged at the airport and I don't want to get a call from The Branch. Right?" said Sharkey his handler.

"You done good Sharks. I will sort you out with the other five G's if this is sweet. Right, next time yeah. I've got to see a man about a dog."

Kusemi got out of the unmarked Police car and drove off in his own car, revenge to the forefront of his mind. He felt a sense of relief that he may be able to do something about his own fate with the Russians and also a dark satisfaction that Daly was going to rue the day he thought he could get away with this. Kusemi on one hand had almost a grudging admiration for Daly's 'bottle' and sheer audacity in doing what he did and if it hadn't been for the Russian problem he may have let Daly get away with a severe beating but in his heart of hearts he knew he couldn't show any sign of weakness. He had to send out a message to his other 'employees' and despite their past, he knew he would have to kill Daly and do so in a way that others would fear ever crossing him. It was the way of the streets, to get respect you had to be feared.

Kusemi made his way to see a contact who would sort him out with a false passport, after which he booked himself onto the first available flight to Palma de Mallorca to take care of business.

Kusemi was born in London of Turkish immigrant parents, who had come to the UK in the 1970's. His mother had two cleaning jobs and his father had been a council road sweeper until his premature death when Kusemi was only five years old. This had affected him greatly and with his mother struggling to make ends meet, he was eventually taken into care and for him on a slippery slope. He had seen his mother work her fingers to the bone and still remained poor. Growing up he vowed he would do whatever it took to make sure he did not have as unfulfilled a life as she had.

He had a problem with authority from an early age and as an only child, living in various care homes, he soon learned how to defend himself. He looked up to a particularly violent child in one home and began to emulate his actions, leading to various stays in young offenders institutions where he further developed his penchant for violence, quickly realising that it earned him a certain kind of respect from his peers.

On the streets he soon got involved in drug dealing, working first for Jamaican Yardies in south London and then setting himself up in this lucrative business, when most of his crew were gunned down in an attack by a rival gang. In his mid twenties he met a girl from a Bermondsey family and she had a son by him, whom they called Mehmet. The relationship soured and he moved out of the family home to a flat where he ran his empire from, but he vowed to look after his son financially and saw him as much as he could, trying to be the father his father never was. Mehmet was what kept him going. Mehmet would have the opportunities that Kusemi never had; the best clothes, the best toys and the best school. Kusemi wanted to keep him oblivious to how he made his money until he was old enough to understand. If Mehmet needed to see him, he would drop everything for him. He was his 'raison d'être'. God help the person who came between him and his son.

Kusemi rang Kingpin and told him to run things while he was away.

"You're in charge until I get back. You're number one, dog. Don't fuck things up 'cos I don't want to be coming looking for you as well," said Kusemi.

"No problem, boss. Leave it to me. Where has he holed up then?" asked Kingpin.

"He's only gone to ground in Majorca, the cheeky bastard!"

"What's the plan then?"

"You know there only is one plan. He crossed the line and I ain't havin' it. He knew there would be consequences when he did it, so he's got to be man enough to take what's due," said Kusemi.

"Do you not want to take me or one of the boys in case he cuts up rough?" asked Kingpin.

"You know me better than that. Do you think I can't handle anything Chas Daly might throw at me?"

"No. I didn't mean it like that boss," interrupted Kingpin nervously, "I just meant it might be less work for you, that's all."

"Thanks, but no thanks. I need you to make sure things run smoothly while I'm gone. Yeah?" said Kusemi.

"Yeah no sweat boss. See you when you get back."

Kusemi came off the phone and threw some clothes into a holdall and set off for the airport with enough money to keep him for a few weeks, if it came to that. He was not going to come home empty-handed. He had a job to do. It would not be the nicest job he had done but it was something he had to do; if he wanted to keep the drug empire he had toiled for over the years and to be top dog in south London. There would always be those in his game who thought they could muscle in on the action unless you had such a fearful reputation that it made them think twice.

Kusemi went to the check-in desk with his booking reference and false passport. He had used the services of his contact before, so he didn't feel overly anxious that his passport might raise suspicion.

He checked in without incident and went to the departure lounge. He still had almost an hour before take off so he deposited himself in an airport lounge bar and ordered a beer. He drained the beer and ordered a second immediately. His thoughts turned to the fact that he would be travelling with the intention of finding and killing someone who, at one stage, he had called a friend. He felt angry that Daly had tried to screw him. After all, Daly knew that he couldn't have done it at a worse time for him, as the money was needed to go to the Russians. Daly knew this and this is why that any thought of letting Daly get away with a good beating evaporated with his anger at Daly's lack of respect in his timing. No time was ever a good time for your second-in-command to try and rip you off to the tune of one million pounds, give or take but this was critical and Daly would have to pay with his life. He cursed Daly for putting him in such a position.

He had had some good times with him. They had stood toe to toe against many who had dared to take them on and he had been a loyal friend for a while. Kusemi wondered whether he had been stealing from him before now. He had trusted Daly with large sums of cash before and he hadn't noticed any going missing, but now he questioned his own judgement of Daly over all those previous years. The final boarding call for his flight came over the tannoy, Kusemi drained his beer and vodka chaser and boarded the plane.

On arrival at Palma airport, Kusemi went to hire a car using his own driving licence. He did not have enough time for his forger to produce a false driving licence and in any case, all he had wanted to do was to avoid Special Branch alerting the authorities that he was leaving the country. He felt that if he went to a foreign car hire firm he would not be noticed. There were numerous car hire firms at the airport, so he picked one he didn't recognise the name of and paid cash instead of using a credit card. He picked up a map of the island and asked the assistant to mark out a route for him to get to the village of Fornalutx. It was now nearly ten o'clock so after changing some Sterling into Euros, Kusemi set off from the airport, as he wanted to find Daly as soon as possible and get back as soon a possible.

Kusemi drove along the motorway looking out for any signposts for Soller but ended up heading into Palma city centre. He spent the next half an hour driving round Palma's Via Centura, which skirts the city, cursing the predicament he found himself in. It was dark, he was driving in a foreign country and he hadn't a clue exactly where he was or exactly where he needed to be. After several near accidents, more by luck than judgement, he saw a sign for Soller, which he recognised as being the name he had been told to head towards. He drove through the tunnel and emerged to eventually locate a sign for Fornalutx. He had been given the full address where it was believed Daly was staying in the village but finding it would be another matter.

He drove into the village, found a parking place in a car park and set off to look for the street he needed. He was aware that he had to be careful Daly didn't see him, as he could end up doing a runner and disappearing for good with no hope of finding him again. He wanted to have the element of surprise on his side. He had been told by his police handler that it was near a small square, so he made his way to a bustling little square full of people that he had passed on his way in. He covertly approached the square and scanned all around. He noted a man with his back to him, sitting at a table with two men and a woman. He couldn't believe his luck. He had found Daly. He would recognise him anywhere, even from behind. Kusemi backtracked and began to search out the street name he was looking for, he stumbled upon it after trying several other streets. He approached the house he had been told was where Daly was staying and pressed down on the door handle. The door opened.

'Fuckin' Muppet,' he said into himself over Daly being stupid enough to leave his front door open. As he entered he was greeted by 'Lamps', Daly's dog that Kusemi knew well. He patted the dog, watching for any signs that someone else was in the house, or in case Daly had returned without him noticing. He checked each of the three floors and found no one in, so he returned to the ground floor and started to look for any sign of his money.

He went to a first floor bedroom that Daly was using and searched any possible hiding place. By the fact that he had seen Daly in the flesh and here was his dog, he had no doubt that this was the right house; but the money could be anywhere. It may not be in the house at all. After a cursory search of each room without success, Kusemi decided to ring Daly's mobile number. Since Daly had disappeared, Kusemi had rung his mobiles on a daily basis. They were still active; he had yet to speak to Daly, but had left him plenty of voicemail messages. He thought he would try again and failing that he would just have to sit tight and wait in the dimly lit house until Daly returned from the square.

He left the house and walked back to the edge of the square. He could still see the back of a seated Daly in the distance. He dialled the number and it rang. To Kusemi's surprise it didn't go onto voicemail, instead he heard a voice he hadn't heard for a few weeks. It was Daly.

8

THE SUN ON MY BACK

"Chas, you stupid paddy Muppet! You fucked up again!" shouted Kusemi, "You thick or what? I told you to put the money in bundles of five grand not two. You just can't get the staff," he laughed towards Kingpin. "Kingpin, leave him to it, let's go to The Admiral, I'm gaspin'. Chas make sure this is sorted; you bollocks and I'll see you tomorrow."

Both Kusemi and Kingpin left shaking their heads in mockery of Daly. Daly wasn't laughing. He was sick of his position being undermined by Kingpin and more and more by Kusemi. He had grown up with Kusemi and had been a loyal foot soldier to him. He had done time for him having been caught in possession of enough cocaine to warrant a charge of supplying and had backed him up in too many fights he cared to remember and this was how he was being treated. Daly had become more and more dissatisfied with his standing. Before Kingpin came along Kusemi had treated him with much more respect. Daly had been through the ringer for him and Kusemi had treated him as a brother. Recently he seemed to be favouring Kingpin over Daly and this belittling of him with Kingpin was making him think about his future.

Daly was born and bred in Bermondsey. He grew up on a large council estate with his mother and half-sister. He never knew his father but his mother told him he had been a traveller from Co. Galway in Ireland. His mother was also of Irish decent but had come over to London after the Second World War looking for work in domestic service, had fallen on hard times and was an alcoholic. She had a second child to another man who wasn't there either for him or his half-sister growing up, so his life of crime and being involved with the Police happened from an early age, which is when he met Kusemi.

He took over the drug dealing in and around The Old Kent Road, when the Yardies gang Kusemi worked for were wiped out in a drive by shooting and Kusemi brought in Daly to run things on the ground for him. They had been inseparable for a while. Danny gave him respect and relied on him and in return he got a good cut of the action. He had given him his all for 15 years and over that time Daly had been respected by other criminals just for being Danny Kusemi's second-in-command or right hand man. Daly could handle himself and had to over the years, to front up for himself and with Danny. He had been shot once in the leg, been stabbed several times and had the scars to prove his loyalty, including two long scars on his cheek, which he received in a pub fight backing up Kusemi over a drug deal gone wrong.

Daly had dished out a few beatings himself. He was no angel but he was getting tired of the lifestyle he had been leading. He was softening with age. He knew that how he made a living was not something to be proud of. It was a career path borne out of necessity. Daly longed to be shot of both Kusemi and Kingpin. London was now stale to him. He drank in the same pub every week, had no true friends, only associates and they were beginning to undermine him. His mother was dead, his half-sister was always off her head on heroin and only came to him looking for drugs and money and he hadn't had a girlfriend for years. The only times he had been truly happy was when he was on holiday with the sun on his back and no-one telling him what to do.

Daly continued into the night, sorting out the cash bundles. As he did so, an idea came into his head. He realised that he had in his possession over one million pounds in cash. This was Kusemi's money; proceeds of an armed robbery and from his drugs importation and distribution. It was money Kusemi needed to bribe the Russian mafia for not seeking retribution against him, after he killed one of them in a bar a few weeks earlier. Kusemi had sought mediation and a deal had been brokered that his life would be spared for one million pounds, to which Kusemi had reluctantly agreed. Kusemi knew that if the Russians wanted him dead he would be dead, so he felt he had no alternative but to pay up.

Daly looked at all the money. Kusemi still trusted him to look after his stash. Daly thought what he could do with that amount of money. It could set him up for life. He could just disappear. He would have to really go underground because for that amount of money Kusemi would hunt him down. Kusemi was vicious and he would kill Daly if he found him. If he did this he could never come back. What had he to come back to? 'Fuck it!' he thought, 'let's do it!'

Daly quickly started putting the cash into the large bin liners he had been given. He brought his car as close to the lock-up garage as he could and he put three bin bags full of cash into his boot. He locked the garage and drove back to his flat. He was fairly calm. He could still change his mind; it wasn't too late. Somehow he didn't think he was going to. All of a sudden he felt good, really good. He felt confident and thought this was something he should have done a long time ago. Danny owed him, big time. He may not see it like that but who cared. As long as Daly got far enough away, where Kusemi had no connections, he'd be fine. He couldn't go to the Costa del Sol or the Costa Blanca because Kusemi had people there who would look for him. He had to go somewhere he wanted to go but where Kusemi would not find him. The Greek islands were out too, as was Tenerife. Anywhere Daly had ever been on holiday was out because he usually went away with Kusemi, who usually met up with ex-associates who now lived in these places. Daly recalled one recent holiday to Majorca with Kusemi when they went to Magaluf. One day when Kusemi was very hung-over, Daly had gone for a drive on his own round part of the island. He had come across a village in the mountains where he had stopped for a drink. It was a different type of place to Magaluf. He had spent a very agreeable afternoon there and thought it was not the sort of place Kusemi would ever dream of looking for him; if he kept his head down. He decided the benefits outweighed the risk, so quickly packed his clothes and transferred the cash into a second suitcase. He fed his faithful companion, 'Lamps', a brown mongrel dog and packed his food and water bowls, ready for his road trip.

Daly's plan was to drive through France and northern Spain in his own car and then to hire a van in Barcelona and get a ferry to Majorca with his dog hidden in the back of the van. He would abandon his car for fear of it giving him away if he brought it to the island. He would then lie low in the village he had visited, either renting or buying a house with his new-found wealth.

He set off driving to the Channel Tunnel, embarking on his new life. There was no turning back. He drove with a sense of gay abandon. He felt this was a new chapter in his life. He had been given a fresh start, albeit it had its own associated risks but he felt these were risks worth taking.

Daly switched off both his mobile phones, as he knew he would be missed later that morning. He drove all through the night and the following day, making regular comfort stops for himself and to allow 'Lamps' to attend to the call of nature. He hired a small van at the port in Barcelona and arrived the next morning, waking up to a view of the port of Palma de Mallorca, as the ferry came in to dock.

After disembarking, he gave 'Lamps' some much needed food, after been cooped up in the van over night and set off in the general direction of the village in the mountains. He knew that by now Kusemi would have worked out that he had stolen the money and be pulling out all the stops to find him.

It was a beautiful summer's day and Daly drove along the motorway looking at place names on the road signs to try and jog his memory of the name of his chosen destination. Noticing a sign for Soller he seemed to remember that the village was beyond this place and headed in the direction of Soller. He eventually stumbled

across a road sign for Fornalutx and he instantly recognised the name as being the village in question, arriving
mid morning. He drove in and made his way to the little
square, which was a hive of activity and sat down at a
café table, ordered a large beer and filled his dog's bowl
full of water from a water fountain. Lamps lapped up
the water in an instant, in one go; such was the heat
of the day. Daly relaxed, enjoying his beer, watching
people coming and going throughout the morning. He
sat behind the relative anonymity his sunglasses offered
him and stayed to enjoy some tapas for lunch, outside
Café sa Plaça. He got chatting to a tall thin waiter from
the café and it soon became clear that there were no
houses in the village available for long-term rental, due
to most being available for short-term holiday lets.
He discovered though that the village had several estate
agents, so Daly decided to take the bull by the horns and
waste no time in looking for somewhere to live.

After spending the afternoon viewing two townhouses with an estate agent, he decided to make an offer
on one without seeing anything further and then turned
to his more pressing requirement of finding a roof over
his and his dog's head until the house purchase could be
completed. He was able to rent the house he was buying
before the sale was complete. Daly paid cash upfront
and moved his suitcases into what would be his future
home. He settled his dog in and decided to go out for
the evening to see what the village and its environs had
to offer.

After several beers in the square being served by his
new acquaintance, who he learnt was called Pepe, and
was from Sweden, Daly was introduced to an American
called Brad. He spent the evening in his company and

the two men drank into the early hours of the morning. As far as his new-found friends were concerned he was Steve from London and he was on holiday.

Over the next couple of weeks Daly settled into his new life and spent most mornings recovering from the excesses of the night before. The village was full of tourists over this period and any initial nervousness he had about being found there soon evaporated and he became very relaxed in his new environment. He had kept his mobiles and over this period had received various messages from Kusemi. The first batch had started off with him pretending to be concerned about his wellbeing. This soon gave way to him stating unequivocally that he was a dead man. Daly could easily get rid of these mobiles and replace them or get new SIM cards but he felt it amusing and took some pleasure in listening to the almost daily diatribe left by Kusemi and Kingpin.

On one balmy evening he was in the plaça drinking with some friends of Brad's when he was introduced to a man who knew Bermondsey. Daly couldn't disguise his London accent and most people he met would have been unfamiliar with his 'manor' so he didn't attempt to hide where he was from but he was surprised to find a man, who had an Irish accent, to have been familiar with Bermondsey. He was even more unnerved to find that this man had been a police officer in his 'manor'. He was ill at ease and without thinking answered his phone whilst at the table, only to discover that he had answered another call from Kusemi without letting it go onto his voicemail as usual.

As Daly answered the call and heard the familiar voice of Kusemi, he moved off from the table and walked towards the water fountain in the plaça. He could have easily just hung up and switched off his phone and returned to his table but he had been thrown off guard by the chance meeting and then this phone call. Before he could mentally develop the idea of whether the Irish man had been sent by Kusemi, he stopped in his tracks.

"I hope you're enjoying that beer. I'm fuckin' paying for it," said Kusemi.

"That was a good guess. I am actually having a beer as it goes."

"I know you are. I can see you at the fountain."

Daly's heart pounded. He looked all around him. Kusemi was watching him but he couldn't see him. His first instinct was to run, to get to his new car parked in the car park and drive to the airport where he had placed the bulk of the cash in a locker but before he could think Kusemi said:

"Don't even think about running. I've got 'Lamps' with me. I've just come from your gaff and I've got your car keys. Not a bad place but then I fuckin' paid for it. All I want is whatever is left. I've managed to buy more time with the Russians. I'm pissed Chas. You know I'm pissed but we can work this out. You are a fuckin' hard man to find but you know me Chas, I always get my man. I want you to come back to your house. We'll talk, just talk and if you haven't pissed all my money away then we can work something out. Got it?" said Kusemi.

Daly was a rat caught in a trap. There was no alternative but to hope that Kusemi would be reasonable with him. He knew he was going to get a beating and in truth, by the code of the streets, he deserved it.

He returned to his table and informed his new acquaintances that he had to return home but that he would be back to finish his beer, although in truth he knew he would not be back that night. His hopes would be restricted to him surviving to see another sunrise.

He walked slowly back past Café Med, where diners were enjoying after diner drinks alfresco, as Daly contemplated what was about to happen. As he turned the corner he saw Kusemi waiting for him. He felt like a naughty school child going in for a caning by his headmaster, although the stakes were much higher.

"So you found me then," he said, as he approached Kusemi.

"Chas, Chas, Chas. You have caused me a lot of grief and there are consequences to that. Let's go indoors and have a chat. You should be more careful, leaving your door unlocked. You never know who might just turn up and walk in."

Both men walked inside and were greeted by 'Lamps' in the entrada. It was evident that Kusemi had spent some time in his house as it had been turned upside down. Daly walked into his living room beyond the entrada and sat down. Kusemi followed and stood beside him.

"What were you thinking of? Did you think I would just lie down and let you screw me for this sort of money?" Kusemi was becoming more animated and Daly could see the veins in his neck start to protrude, as he could no longer hide his anger.

"How am I supposed to go back without you in a fuckin' body bag? It would put me in a very bad position. I've looked out for you, given you a good piece of the action for years, trusted you and this is how you repay me."

Kusemi moved towards Daly and punched him hard to the jaw. Daly stood up, reeling from the blow.

"Look let's sort this out without a dust up 'cos if you hit me again I ain't gonna take it and you and I will really fall out," said Daly, spitting some blood onto the floor.

"Where's my fuckin' money?" said Kusemi.

"It's not here. I have it in a safe place. I can get it for you. I have to be honest I've spent some of it buying this place but I can sell it, no problem," said Daly, watching Kusemi for any sign he was carrying a knife or other weapon.

"Where exactly is my money?" asked Kusemi, "I'm beginning to fuckin' lose my patience."

"It's in a locker at the airport. I've got the key…" Daly paused as he realised the locker key which he had deposited in his cigarette packet, was not in his possession, as he had left his cigarette packet back at the table where he had been drinking.

"Listen, the key is in my fag packet. I've left it with a guy back at my table. You'll not believe me when I tell you he's ex-Old Bill from Rotherhithe. Straight up, James something. He's a paddy, about 40, lives in the village. I swear, come on I'll get it," said Daly, moving towards the door.

Kusemi lifted a table lamp from a coffee table pulling it with enough effort to separate it from its flex and hit Daly on the back of his head with force, knocking him to the floor. Daly curled up into the foetal position, as a reign of kicks was directed at his midriff. Soon after he lost consciousness and with it any hope of his new life in the sun.

9

AN EYE FOR AN EYE

James wakened with a sense of purpose on Monday morning. This was D-Day for several reasons. Firstly it was Adam's first day at his new school in Palma but also James was to meet with Inspector Martinez later that day and he was going to disclose to him his full or almost full knowledge of the key and locker, which he had told Martinez about during his last telephone conversation over the weekend. The plan was to get to Adam's new school after breakfast and for James to then drive to Palma airport and return the cash in the brown leather holdall to the locker before going and see Martinez at Soller Police station. The only way James felt he could cover his back was to tell Martinez that he had discovered the locker, looked inside but never actually removed the holdall. His conscience was clear as far as taking any money was concerned, so a little white lie to protect him and his family, he could live with.

James walked to the corner shop in the plaça, once up and dressed. Thankfully, the village was back to normal, save for the remains of tissue paper bunting and the last of the bottles being cleared away by the

Council refuge collectors, who had obviously been working since dawn to clear away the mountain of litter that the three day fiesta produced. James was in a pensive frame of mind. As he climbed the steps leading up to his street, he surveyed the view. He felt so privileged that this place was home to him. Just the simple things gave him pleasure, the mere fact that he could step out of his house, walk along a cobbled street, usually in glorious sunshine, pause at the top of a set of steps to admire a jaw-droppingly majestic vista, never failed to thrill him. After taking in the view he could amble down to get most of his daily requirements at a little shop, or stop off and have a coffee in the beautiful little plaça, before sauntering back the few metres home; these simple pleasures were priceless. On reflection, he paused and vowed that neither Kusemi nor his own brief flirt with appropriating the money would stand in his way of these simple pleasures being prematurely curtailed.

Adam was up and in his new school uniform when he returned home from the shop.

"Well. A new chapter of your life is about to begin. You'll meet lots of new people and make lots of new friends. This is an exciting time for you. Are you looking forward to it?" asked James.

"I'm a little nervous but excited at the same time, if you know what I mean. Does this uniform look alright on me?" asked Adam, looking at himself in the mirror.

"What a handsome boy! Or should I say young man?" said James.

"Dad! Don't say that," said an awkward Adam.

"Let's get breakfast. I don't want you to be late on your first day. You don't want to keep all those girls waiting, do you?" said James smiling.

"Dad! Stop it!" said Adam.

After breakfast James went next door and recovered the brown leather holdall and placed the cash inside it, before concealing the bag in the bin liner again. He met Adam at the front door of the house and he kissed Charlotte and his son Reuben goodbye and both father and son set off for the car park.

"Good luck! Both of you!" shouted Charlotte from the doorstep.

"Thanks mum," responded Adam, as the pair continued. "What's in the bin bag Dad?" asked Adam curiously.

"Oh, nothing much. Just three-quarters of a million pounds in cash, that's all," said James in a sarcastic way.

"Yeah, right Dad," responded Adam.

James drove the 40km route to Adam's new school and took him in, wanting to see for himself the environment in which he would be in for next number of years. The school was an International school with a mixture of English- speaking kids, Mallorcan kids with the odd German as well, but the curriculum was taught in English. Reuben was to start school the next week but he would be attending the local school in Fornalutx, where classes were taught mostly in Catalan. It was felt that Adam was too old to be thrown into a Mallorcan school and anyway he would still learn Castilian Spanish. He met one of Adam's new teachers and when he turned, he could see Adam already in conversation with several of his new classmates, so content that his son was already fitting in, he slipped off with a wave and a wink to his son.

James' thoughts now turned to the other matter in hand. He drove to Palma airport once more and parked the car. He retrieved the bag in the bin liner from the boot. He made the now familiar journey on foot to the locker and deposited the bag inside, removing the bin bag and re-securing the locker before walking back to his car. 'Job done,' he thought as he got in.

He set off on route for Soller police station. He arrived in Soller and parked his car in a car park. It was a busy Monday morning in the town. The local schools had not started back after the summer recess and there were still quite a few holiday-makers milling around or sitting outside the numerous cafés that surrounded the plaça. It was such a beautiful morning and to compose his thoughts, James decided to have a coffee in the square. In any case he would have to phone Inspector Martinez to make sure he could see him before just turning up at the station. Whilst sipping the last of his coffee his mobile phone rang.

"Hello."

"Is that Mr Gordon, Adam Gordon's father?" said a woman's voice.

"Yes. Who is speaking?" asked a bemused James.

"This is Linda Taylor, the Administrator at The Belfry School. I was asked to ring you by Miss Blanchford; Adam's new form teacher. I'm afraid she is new and didn't follow the correct school procedures…"

"I'm sorry, I'm not with you," interrupted James, "procedures for what?"

"Well I'm not sure what has happened here but this morning about half an hour ago a man came to the school and asked to take your son Adam out of school. He said there had been a car accident involving you and your wife and that you were both in hospital and that your injuries were life threatening. He told

Miss Blanchford that he was a British police officer on secondment with the Guardia Civil Traffic Department and he produced some form of photo identification to show he was a police officer. Well, she allowed Adam to go with this man before it occurred to her to inform this office. We obviously would not have released your son without at least having attempted to make contact with both your wife and you first, which is what I am doing. Have you been involved in an accident this morning?"

"No I have not. Let me get this straight. You say that half an hour ago a man walked into your school, went to the classroom where my son was and told his teacher that both his parents had been in a car accident and she just let this man take my son. Are you kidding me?" shouted James, as the realisation of what had just happened hit him. "I only left him there an hour ago. What did this man look like?"

"Hold on please, I have Miss Blanchford and the Head Teacher with me. I'll ask."

There was a pause and James could hear muffled voices at the other end of the phone.

"OK, he was about 35-40 years of age, was well-built, had a shaved head and spoke with a London accent apparently."

James' fears had just been realised. The description, although a little vague was describing Kusemi. It was now obvious to James that Kusemi must have followed them to the school and once James had left, he seized his opportunity in taking Adam, doubtless in an effort to get his money back.

"Mr Gordon can you confirm that you did not give authority to this man to collect Adam. If this is the case we must inform the Police immediately."

James was trying hard to think. Kusemi had kidnapped his son. He would probably try to make contact with him shortly. If the Police became involved it may compromise his son's safety.

"Right… I think I know what has happened," said James slowly in an effort to quickly try to formulate a plausible lie.

"My wife was involved in a minor car accident this morning. It would appear that its severity has been lost in translation. Don't worry there is no need to contact the Police. I will go to the Police Station myself, which is where Adam is. It's fine. I'm sorry I know what has happened. Thank you for calling. Good-bye."

James hung up before there were any more awkward questions. He wasn't sure if he had done enough to allay their fears or whether they would contact the local Police anyway. He had to think. His world was spiralling out of control, his head was spinning and he felt nauseous. He threw some coins on the table and ran back to his car. He drove at speed back to Fornalutx and abandoned his car in the car park and ran up to his house. Charlotte and Reuben were out. This would be the only point of reference that Kusemi would have to contact him unless Adam could give him his mobile number.

James had suffered loss before. He knew what it felt like to be scared, he had been no stranger to trials, tribulations and disillusionment, but this feeling of total helplessness and despair was completely alien to him. Despair soon gave way to an all-encompassing rage within him, both at the dire situation he found himself in and at his own stupidity in putting his son in harm's way. A psychopathic killer had kidnapped his son Adam and he had over £730,000 of this man's drug money.

His 'Garden of Eden' here in his beloved Mallorca was beginning to be spoiled by the grim underbelly of the dark side of life.

James stayed in his bedroom, pacing up and down with his mobile phone on the bed looking at it, almost commanding it to ring. How could he get his son back unharmed? Should he go to the Police? Surely he must? How could he tell his wife? He had no way of contacting Kusemi. How would Kusemi make contact with him, as he surely must in order to get his money back? Would Adam remember their home telephone number? James sat down on the bed to try to clear his random questions and to think. The facts were that Kusemi had clearly known that James had got his hands on his money through his chance meeting with Daly, whom Kusemi had murdered. He had seen Kusemi in Fornalutx on two occasions so he obviously knew James and his family lived there. He had come home one night and he had the feeling that someone had been in his house so he took it for granted that Kusemi knew where he lived. He had an idea of the make, model and colour of the hire car he had been driving, but it would have probably have been changed by now. His friend and still serving Police Sergeant in Rotherhithe CID, Bam Bam was knowledgeable on Kusemi. "That's it!" thought James.

He couldn't wait around for Kusemi to make contact with him. He would ring Bam Bam and see if he could get a mobile number for Kusemi. James knew that Bam Bam was coming to Mallorca later that day to assist the local Police in the murder enquiry but he had no time to lose.

He rang the Rotherhithe CID office.

"CID Rotherhithe, can I help you?" said a female.

"Can I speak to Bam Bam? It's James Gordon and tell him it's urgent," said James.

"I'm sorry he's not in today. Can I help?"

"I used to work with Bam Bam and I'm ex-Old Bill, probably before your time but I need to speak to him urgently. I haven't got his mobile number to hand and I know he's coming to Mallorca today. Can you give me his mobile number or at least ring him and ask him to ring me on this number as a matter of urgency?"

"I can get him to ring you. Give me your number and did you say your name was James?"

"Just tell him to ring Semtex on this number urgently."

"No problem I'll do it straight away."

James hung up and began pacing the floor holding the phone in his hand willing it to ring and making sure he had a clear signal. Two minutes seemed like two hours but his mobile rang and he answered on the first ring.

"Hello Bam Bam?" he asked anxiously.

"Semtex what's up?" came the familiar voice of Detective Sgt Wiggins.

"Bam Bam, thank God! Listen I need your help. Kusemi has kidnapped my son. I need to contact him. Have you got a mobile number for him?" said James breathing deeply.

"Well I have several numbers for him but he changes them all the time. I can get them for you and get back to you. Hang on, I know who his handler is: Chris Sharkey. He's bad news. We think he has been on Kusemi's payroll for years but he covers his tracks well. Do you want me to contact him and ask for his up to date mobile or would that compromise things?"

"No, just do it and ring me as soon as you can. I'm in bits here mate. Charlotte doesn't know he's got Adam yet. I've been a fool but that's for another time."

"I'll sort it. I'll ring you as soon as I can. Have you told Martinez yet?"

"No I want to try to speak to Kusemi first."

"Right, well we'll speak soon."

James lay back on his bed with some relief. At least someone else now knew the situation. He just hoped he could get to speak to Kusemi before he hurt his son. He must be in a dreadful state, thought James. He vowed that if Kusemi harmed his son he would hunt him down to exact revenge. His phone rang again.

"Right. It's me. Have you got a pen?" asked Bam Bam.

"Fire away."

Bam Bam gave James a mobile number belonging to Kusemi and said,

"I had to tell Sharkey why I wanted it otherwise he wouldn't have given it to me, so doubtless he will contact Kusemi as we're speaking to tell him to expect your call. How the hell did he get Adam and what does he want?" he asked.

"I located his money stash and I was taking it to Martinez but I had to get Adam to school. Kusemi called for him saying we had been in a traffic accident. He had obviously been watching me and followed us to the International School this morning. I'll tell you, if he so much as hurts a hair on his head, I'll not be held responsible for my actions."

"Look I know how you must be feeling but for Adam's sake you must remain calm and think about what you are doing. The most important thing is to get your son home safe and sound. Let's worry about what happens to Kusemi after that. I'm going to get in to Palma at about 3 pm today so I'll meet you straight off the flight. In the meantime try the number and ring me back with what he says. Ok?"

"Ok. Thanks I owe you," said James in a more calm way.

He hung up and paused to take a deep breath before dialling Kusemi's mobile number. It rang.

"Yeah," said a male in a London accent. James gathered himself instantaneously.

"Danny Kusemi? You have something belonging to me. My name is James Gordon. Do you know who I am?"

"Yeah I know who you are and you have something belonging to me."

"The first thing I want to know is that you have not harmed my son, because if you have or if you hurt him in any way I will not let the Police take care of you, make no mistake I will find you, I will get to you and your death will be very slow. Do we understand each other? Now let me speak to my son," said James, trying to remain calm.

"Who says I've got your son?" said Kusemi.

"Look! If you want your money and you don't want the Police involved, I will not give you a penny until I know my son is OK. Now let me speak to him."

There was a short silence and James could hear the sound of a door being opened and then he heard the beautiful sound of his son's voice.

"Hello."

"Adam! It's Dad." James began to well up, a combination of relief and joy that his son was still alive and anger at Kusemi and himself for putting this innocent in danger.

"Adam, are you alright? Has the man hurt you?"

"I'm OK. I'm scared Dad. What's happening? I want to come home."

Kusemi came back onto the phone;

"Right we've established he's alive, for now anyway. Now you listen to me. This is what I want. You will go to Festival Park Shopping Centre. Do you know the retail park outside of Palma?" asked Kusemi.

"Yes I know it," snapped James, having difficulty keeping his anger in check.

"Go to the toilet block at the far end of the shops, the block with offices above it; tomorrow at 10 am. Bring the money with you in a holdall. Go into the first cubicle as you enter the male toilets with the bag. Place the bag on the floor and lock the door. Then climb out over the top and walk outside. When you come outside there will be a silver van in the car park in the last parking space beside the exit. Walk to within 50 feet of this van but do not go any closer. If you have not screwed up, your boy will then be released unharmed. If you do screw up you will never see you boy alive again. Do you understand?"

"I'm not happy with this. What is to stop you from collecting the money and still killing my boy? No, I want the hand over face to face and I want to see my son present at the hand-over," said James.

"I'm fuckin' running the show here!" shouted Kusemi.

"You do it my way or I start sending you body parts through the post. This is not a fuckin' joke. If you hadn't taken my money the boy wouldn't have been involved. Be there tomorrow. No Old Bill or the boy is dead. No show the boy is dead. No money or not all the money the boy is dead. Do I make myself clear?"

James did not want to anger Kusemi. He held all the aces and he had his son. Adam's safety was the most important factor right now.

"Ok I'll be there. Make sure my son is not hurt. He is frightened. Do not do anything to worsen the situation," said James.

The line then went dead. Kusemi had hung up.

James slumped onto the bed with his head in his hands. The enormity of the situation hit him like a sledgehammer. James sat in quiet contemplation with all his thoughts on his son Adam. He contemplated trying to get a trace on Kusemi's position by informing Police and ringing him back but he knew Kusemi would have switched off that mobile and he didn't have much time. Suddenly he sat bolt upright. James rang Bam Bam's mobile number as an idea came into his head like a bolt from the blue. It was a bold idea and one of a desperate man but he thought it might just work.

"Hello."

"Bam Bam. It's James. Where are you?" asked James.

"I'm on my way to the airport. Is everything Ok? Did you speak to Kusemi?" he asked concerned.

"I did. He wants a hand over tomorrow but I don't trust him. I need something from you. Does Kusemi have any family?"

"He has an ex-partner and a son who is about 10 or 11 years old. Why? Where are you going with this?"

"What I'm going to tell you, you might not like but the life of my son is at stake and this is the only way

I feel I can get the leverage I need. Do you know where his son lives?"

"Listen Semtex I can't be party to anything illegal, you know me better than that. What are you proposing?"

"I wouldn't ask unless I thought it would save my son's life. You know what I'm going to do. I'm going to fight fire with fire; an eye for an eye. I'm going to go to London and use his son as leverage. You don't need to know anything else. All I need is a name, description and an address. Come on Bam Bam, do you think I'm going to do anything other than take the kid for a ride in the car for a few hours?"

"I hope you bloody well know what you are doing. You will owe me big style for this and I will only give you this information if you swear that nothing happens to his boy."

"You know I wouldn't harm him."

"I know, I know. Right, his son is Mehmet. He lives with Kusemi's ex-partner Jackie Piper. He goes to Blackheath School and the last time I saw him he had short black hair and was a typical looking sprouting young man. He has the look of his father about him but that's all I can say. He lives with his mum at 24 Rotherhithe New Road, you know the new development of town houses there?"

"Yeah I know them," said James.

"What's your plan?" asked Bam Bam.

"I haven't really got one. This just came to me and I've rung you," said James.

"You could always do it by the book and get Martinez involved. He could have an undercover unit at the exchange..."

"No," interrupted James, "I have a feeling that Kusemi does not want any loose ends. I can't take any risks when it comes to the life of my son. This is the only way I think he will release Adam unharmed. By the way does he get on with his son?"

"This is why I think you might have the leverage you need. Kusemi dotes on his son Mehmet. He would do anything for him. Jackie and he have little to do with each other anymore but he loves his son big time."

"Right, well I need to get a flight out of here ASAP. By the way I appreciate this," said James.

"What's going to happen at the meet then?"

"What I want you to do for me, is to keep Martinez out of this until early tomorrow morning. Once I have Kusemi's son I will ring you. The hand over is to take place in the gent's toilets at an out of town retail park called Festival Park. Martinez will know it.

The plan is to take a holdall with the money I recovered and at 10 am to place it in the first cubicle and to lock the door and then climb over the wall of the cubicle. He states that a silver van will then be outside in a parking space beside the exit to the car park. He will then release Adam when he has got the money.

If you want to get things arranged so that local Police can be in place but they are not to do anything until I know Adam is safe. If he sees Police he has threatened to kill Adam. You know as well as I do that he is capable of it. He knows what I look like but I am going to get a friend of mine to do the drop off. He doesn't know it yet but he's going to have to be me in the morning. Have you got all that? I don't want any mistakes," said James firmly.

"I've got it but what do you mean the money you recovered?" asked Bam Bam.

"Don't worry about that now," said James.

"OK. If I need anything else I will ring you. Good Luck. Keep me posted."

James came off the phone and grabbed his passport and threw a change of clothes into a bag and went onto his computer. There was a flight from Palma to Stansted in a few hours, which he booked. He still had some loose ends to tie up, so he rang his friend Matt.

"Hi Matt it's James. I need to see you urgently. Can you come to the house straight away? I'll explain everything when I see you." asked James bluntly.

"Yeah of course. I'll be there in ten minutes," replied Matt.

Whilst waiting for Matt's imminent arrival, James drew breath to build himself up for a call he could no longer put off making. He rang Charlotte's number and waited for her response.

"Hi. Have you been to see the Police yet?" she asked forthrightly.

"Charlotte where are you?"

"I'm just at Alcampo getting some food shopping. Why?" she said nervously.

"Right, I don't want you to freak out but I need you to listen very carefully to what I say. OK?" said James slowly.

"OK but you are already scaring me. What is it?" asked Charlotte anxiously.

"As you know I was going to the Police station with the locker key after I got Adam to school. Well, I got a call from the school to say they had let him be taken by a man purporting to be a Police officer on secondment with The Guardia Civil. The school were told that we had been in a car accident and were in the accident and emergency at hospital. The school claimed that he had photo ID showing he was a police officer but the description is that of Kusemi. I now know he has got Adam."

James could hear Charlotte breaking down on the other end of the phone.

"Listen. I have spoken to Adam a few minutes ago. He's alright. He hasn't been hurt. You have got to be strong for Adam's sake." said James, trying to give Charlotte a crumb of comfort.

"How can I be strong when a murderer has kidnapped our son," sobbed Charlotte, "I can't believe you have been so stupid to get involved in all this."

"Ok! I'm trying to get our son back, so you must listen to me. I am flying to London in a few hours. I have got the address of Kusemi's son. I am going to take him in the morning. It's the only way. I need a strong bargaining position. Bam Bam will be in Mallorca in a few hours. I will leave you his number. I can't risk the local Police cocking this up. Don't worry I will get Adam back if it's the last thing I do. Come home now and take it easy driving. I'll be away by the time you get back. Listen, it will be alright. I love you."

A short time later Matt arrived at the door.

"Come in. Take a seat. Where do I start? OK, I don't have long so I will have to give you the bare bones. I know who killed Daly. It's a guy called Danny Kusemi. He's in Mallorca and he's kidnapped Adam," started James.

"What?" asked a bemused Matt, looking up.

"I found a key in the cigarette packet belonging to Daly which opened a locker in Palma airport which contained a holdall with a substantial amount of cash. He has worked out that I have this money, which I have, but I was going to tell the Police in Soller about today. Before I could do this Kusemi kidnapped Adam. I need you to put a baseball cap on and one of my shirts and go to Festival Park tomorrow at 10am and place this holdall in the first cubicle of the gent's toilets at the far end. You know the ones, we have used them in the past."

"Yeah I know them. I just can't quite get my head round this," said Matt.

"I know but we don't have time. Once you do this and for God's sake don't lose the bag, lock the door and climb over the cubicle wall and walk out. There should be, by then, a silver van parked beside the exit. I assume Kusemi will wait until you go into the toilet before bringing in the silver van. You have to walk towards this van but are not to go any closer than about 50 feet. At this stage Adam is to be released. This will allow him time to check the money.

The problem is that I don't trust the guy. So I am flying to London tonight to kidnap his son as a bargaining chip. Keep your mobile on at all times. I need to be able to contact you. A Detective friend of mine has been informed of the hand-over and if I can get Kusemi's son he will be at the drop with local Police, out of sight. You shouldn't even know they are there. I'm sorry to put you in this position but I need you. Adam's life is at stake here. Kusemi has threatened to kill him if he doesn't get this money. I couldn't care less what happens to him afterwards as long as we get Adam back safely. Are you up for this?" asked James.

"You can count on me. I'll do my bit; just make sure you know what you're doing in London," said Matt.

"If I have to serve a prison sentence to get my son back I'll do it. I've been a bit foolish over this and I just want to make it right. I can do it so that his boy is not going through what Adam is going through now. Right, I've got to go to the airport.

"I need you to follow me in your car. Charlotte knows what has happened. She's not in great shape. Right, here's a shirt and a baseball cap. He knows what I look like but I think he'll be watching from a distance and you look enough like me. The main thing is the money bag. I will retrieve it from the locker for you. Don't even have a peek. I don't want to find out you've done a runner with it," said James trying in vain to force a wry smile.

"Good luck," said Matt, shaking James by the hand.

"Likewise. I'll see you in the Departures terminal in half an hour," said James and with that Matt left and a short time later James drove to the airport in preparation of committing an arrestable offence, for which if convicted he could be spending a few years at Her Majesty's Pleasure.

On arrival, he quickly parked the car and walked to the locker area of the terminal, where Matt was waiting.

"Right, this is it," said James, opening locker 27 and handing Matt the brown leather holdall full of cash.

"Remember what I said. Don't even have a peak at it and good luck for tomorrow. Right, I'd better get my flight."

"You can count on me. Everything will be alright," said Matt, as James made his way to catch his flight to London.

10

NO GREATER LOVE

James hurriedly made his way to the check-in desk, onwards through security and on down to his departure gate. The airport was busy with the hoards of holiday-makers, returning to the four corners of the world after a fortnight in the sun. Everyone was tanned and relaxed. There were the perennial sombreros being worn mostly by those heading back to Britain and Ireland. Their lives seemed so uncomplicated in comparison to the situation that he now found himself in.

His thoughts were never far from his son Adam and what he must be going through. He tried not to dwell on it as when he did, he visibly became distressed and he didn't want to draw attention to his plight. James busied himself with trying to plan what exactly he would do when he got to Stansted. Firstly he would hire a car and drive to Rotherhithe. He would get there for about 1am. He would familiarise himself with both the house where Kusemi's son Mehmet lived with his mother and make sure he knew exactly where Blackheath School was. His plan was that if he had an opportunity to take Mehmet outside his house, then this is where he would try to take him. If there was no opportunity here he would, in almost a mirror image to what Kusemi had done, go to this school and purport to being a serving Police officer needing to take Mehmet out of school, for a reason James had yet to think sufficiently plausible.

He had brought with him his old Metropolitan Police warrant card, which he had kept as a memento of his days as a serving officer and may just come in handy in the circumstances. The best place to take the boy may be as he was dropped off at school but one thing was sure, he would not leave empty-handed. The life of his own son depended on this, he felt.

Although tired from the stresses of the day and his travelling, James could not afford to sleep. If he missed his opportunity he would never forgive himself and he had very little time to pull this off. The drop-off was at 10am local time in Mallorca, which was 9am GMT, so he had no time to waste, especially if he couldn't get Mehmet until he got to his school.

The instruction to board his flight came over the public address system and James joined the queue and boarded the plane. He closed his eyes for most of the flight trying to sleep but it evaded him. He persisted with shutting his eyes in an effort to avoid having to make small talk to the woman next to him, who at every possible opportunity attempted to engage him in conversation about whether he had enjoyed his holiday and about how she had missed her two cats.

He was in no mood for listening to the ravings of a lonely, middle-aged divorcee but he couldn't bring himself to be rude or abrupt, so at least with his eyes closed he could temporarily escape.

The plane touched down on time and James breathed a sigh of relief to have escaped from 'his captor' and went to hire a car. He drove into London and decided to first go to Blackheath where he had fond memories, having lived there when first married. It was an oasis of calm, which seemed a million miles away from the built-up, deprived inner city areas of Lewisham, Deptford and New Cross but was, in truth, surrounded by them. It was one of the few areas of southeast London that had so much green open space. Set beside Greenwich Park and with some notable Georgian and Victorian architecture James was sorry to be back in such circumstances.

He made his way to where he thought the school was and was content to find that he was correct. He drove around the area, recalling places and times spent. The area was quiet. It was now 2.30 am and the only cars on the road were a few Hackney carriages, the odd Police car and a van with the morning newspapers being delivered to newsagents from the printers at Wapping.

James decided he needed to make sure of exactly what house on Rotherhithe New Road was his target address, so he drove the few miles there and satisfied himself he had got the right house and parked his car in a position which would not draw attention from a potential passing Police car, nor from any residents inside but with a good view of the front door.

He settled down for the rest of the night, reclined in his driver's seat listening to the radio in an effort to stay awake. Dawn eventually came and so started just another day in the life of a busy capital city.

The first sign of life from within the property came just after 8am, when someone drew back the front curtains on the first floor. James wished he had been more organised and brought a pair of binoculars or even his camera with a zoom lens. At least he had his glasses; otherwise he would really have had a problem. The ground floor curtains were the next to be drawn back and James for the first time caught a glimpse of his target, or who at least he thought was Mehmet.

There was a bus stop about 50 yards from the front door which would give him a better view, so he got out and stood with several other people at the bus stop watching for any sign that the occupants of his target address were coming out. A bus pulled up and everyone at his stop got on, leaving him all alone. As the bus drove off, he looked back at the house to find a woman and a boy fitting the description of Mehmet already outside and walking towards a black BMW car parked outside the house. There was no chance here so he quickly ran back to his hire car and managed to follow the BMW from a safe distance. It was now almost 8.25am. As he drove towards Blackheath, the traffic got heavy and his biggest fear was that Mehmet was going to be late for school and that he may not get him in time for the hand-over at 9am. His mobile phone rang. It was Bam Bam.

"Bam Bam, I'm driving so make it quick," said James hurriedly.

"Right, well I took the liberty of informing Martinez about the drop-off. I met him this morning and I felt he could be trusted not to screw things up. I am at Festival Park with him and several officers from another unit.

He didn't want to use the local officers as you thought someone may have been giving information to Kusemi. We're well dug in here so he shouldn't know. Your mate knows where to go, doesn't he?"

"Yes he knows," said James.

"How are things at your end?" asked Bam Bam.

"I'm tailing Mehmet and his mum. We're stuck in traffic in Deptford. I hope we're not too late. I'm going to try to get him outside the school," said James.

"Look I can get uniform to stop the car and at least bring Mehmet to the station and give you some access to him just to get Kusemi to believe you've got him."

"No it's too late for that. Look I have to go, the traffic is moving. I don't want to miss them at the lights."

James was conscious of the fact that if he was left sitting at the traffic lights he could quite easily miss his best chance to get Mehmet. He could easily get blocked in. He had forgotten just how aggressive and discourteous London drivers were, especially during rush hour.

James could hear sirens from behind getting closer. It was an ambulance battling to get through the traffic with its 'blues and twos' on. This enabled him to get directly behind the target vehicle, which had pulled in to allow the ambulance to pass. James breathed a sigh of relief and was now beginning to sweat from the lack of sleep and the concentration required to stop people trying to push in from all directions. He would not allow any vehicle to get in between at this stage. They were now about a mile from the school. It was going to be down to the wire on timing. The BMW finally pulled up outside the entrance to the school and Mehmet got out and started to walk through the school gate. James quickly got out of his car, which he left running and shouted to Mehmet to stop. The boy turned, startled as James ran towards him reaching into his pocket to find his old Police warrant card.

"Mehmet can I have a word. I am DC Gordon from Rotherhithe CID. Your father Danny Kusemi has been arrested and he has asked to speak to you urgently. Can you come with me? It's very important," said James.

"What's happened? Why has he been arrested?" he asked.

"Look I'll explain everything as we drive. We haven't much time. I'll contact your school and your mum in a little while but we need to go."

"OK," said Mehmet timidly.

Mehmet followed James to his car and James guided him into the rear of the car and drove off. He drove the short distance to the open heath area of Blackheath and pulled in. It was 10.02am in Mallorca.

"Wait here. I need to ring your dad," said James as he got out of the car.

He rang Kusemi's mobile number.

"Yeah?" came the answer.

"Kusemi. It's James Gordon. Where is my son?"

"He's safe. I can see you. Hang on that's not you. You are on a mobile. What's going on? Have you left my money where I told you?" asked Kusemi, who was obviously in sight of his friend Matt.

"Listen very carefully to me. The money is where you told me to put it, except I got a friend of mine to put it there. You can probably see him, wearing a blue shirt and a baseball cap. Can you see him?" asked James.

"Yeah I see him," said Kusemi.

"Well I want you to go to the toilet cubicle and stay on the line. Start walking."

"OK. I'm walking towards it. There had better be no funny business or your boy's dead," said Kusemi, obviously agitated.

There was a pause but James could hear a door open and heard Kusemi sliding out the bag from under the cubicle door and he heard the sound of a zip opening.

"Right, well most of it seems to be here," said Kusemi.

"I want you to release my son immediately and give him to my friend who you saw outside and just so there is no mistake I want you to know that I am in London and I have your son Mehmet with me. If you don't release my son or if you have harmed him, I will do exactly the same to your son. I'll get him for you," said James as he opened the car door and pushed the mobile towards Mehmet, holding it up to him.

"It's your dad on the phone. Just say hello to him."

"Dad where are you? What's going on?" said Mehmet, before James pulled the mobile away from Mehmet and closed the car door.

"Right, now you know I'm not fucking about. You release my son NOW!" shouted James.

Mehmet looked at him from within the car, so James locked the car having previously put on the child locks. He seemed concerned by the shouting.

"If you fuckin' hurt one hair on his head I will kill your boy, your wife and anyone else you care about. Only then will I come for you and you will die a very slow death," said Kusemi aggressively.

"I will give you one minute to get my son into the hands of my friend and the clock is ticking. Once he is with my friend I will release your son. DO IT!" shouted James.

James could hear Kusemi walking again and after a short time he could hear the sound of something being opened like a van door. He could hear some muffled sounds and then heard him say "Go to him."

"Right it's done. He's with your friend. Let my son go," said Kusemi.

"I will ring my friend and if he confirms he has my son I will let Mehmet go. I will ring you back."

James hung up and rang Matt's mobile.

"Matt it's me. Have you got Adam?" he asked anxiously.

"Yeah I've got him. He's OK. He's a little bit shaken but he doesn't appear to have been physically harmed. I'm taking him back to my car and I'll drive him straight back to Charlotte," said Matt.

"Let me speak to him," said James.

"Hello," said Adam.

"Thank God, Adam. Listen are you OK? Did that man hurt you?" asked James.

"I'm OK now. I just want to get home. He really scared me Dad. I thought he was going to kill me."

"I know, I know. It's over now. I'm going to make this better when I get home. Matt is going to take you home to mum. I will see you tonight. Put Matt back on."

"Hi it's me again," said Matt.

"Listen get Adam out of there. The Police are waiting for Kusemi. I don't want him to try and get him back," said James.

"We're in the car now," said Matt.

"Thanks Matt. I owe you one. I'll see you tonight all being well."

James hung up and immediately rang Bam Bam's mobile.

"Hi James. I have seen Adam get into a car with your friend. I've got Kusemi in my sights. Are we good to go?" asked Bam Bam.

"Yeah, get the bastard," said James hanging up.

James turned towards his hire car where he could see the frightened face of Kusemi's son looking out at him. James unlocked the door and got into the driver's seat and turned round to look at Mehmet.

"Mehmet, I've something to tell you. I haven't been totally honest with you but it was for a very good reason. There are things I'm going to need to tell you but I want to ask you a couple of questions first. Do you know what your dad does for a living?" asked James.

"Well I think he's a property developer or something. I know some of my friends at school say things like he's a criminal and stuff like that. Why? And why where you shouting at my dad?" asked Mehmet.

"Firstly Mehmet I am no longer a police officer. I used to be in Rotherhithe but I now live in Mallorca in Spain. I have a boy about the same age as you and I love him very much. A friend of your dad's came to live in my village, a man called Chas Daly. Do you know him?" asked James.

"Yeah I know Chas."

"Well this might come as a shock and you might not believe me but you're going to find this out for yourself soon enough. Your dad is not a very nice man. He has done some very bad things. Your dad imports illegal drugs and Chas took a lot of money from your dad. Your dad killed Chas for this and he then kidnapped my son, Adam. He threatened to kill my son, which is why I needed you to come with me this morning. I'm not going to hurt you. I'm going to take you back to your mum now," said James.

"I don't believe you. My dad wouldn't do that," said Mehmet, clearly distressed at what James had said.

"I don't expect you to believe me but ask your mum about what he does. As far as him murdering Chas Daly goes, he is being arrested for that as we speak. I'm sorry you had to hear it like this from me but you're better off without him, he's bad news son."

James drove Mehmet back to Rotherhithe New Road and both he and Mehmet went to his front door. The black BMW was outside and James rang the doorbell. The woman he had seen earlier came to the door.

"Mehmet, what are you doing home? What's happened? Who are you?" she asked, clearly puzzled. Mehmet ran to her and hugged her.

"He says that dad is a criminal and that he has killed Chas," said Mehmet crying.

"What! Who the fuck are you?" said his mother with disdain towards James.

"I think this would be better done inside. I mean you no harm. I used to be a Detective round here and I have only done what I had to, to save my boy from Danny Kusemi. Please may I come in?" asked James in a soft tone.

Mehmet's mother paused, looking James up and down and decided he didn't seem to pose her a threat.

"Right come in but you had better have a good reason for filling my son's head full of lies," she said taking a step back to allow James to come inside. They went into the kitchen and stood.

"I had no other choice than to tell Mehmet what his father does because of what has happened. I now live in Mallorca but I used to work with Bam Bam, who I think you know.

"A man moved into my village and he gave me something without realising it. That man was Chas Daly. Chas took a lot of Danny's drug money and did a runner and Danny came looking for him.

"The night I met Chas he got a phone call from Danny and he went to meet him. I found Chas dead the next day. Danny then came looking for me, as he knew I had found his money, which I was in the process of handing into the local police, before you get any ideas. He kidnapped my 11-year-old son and threatened to kill him. The only way I felt I could protect my son was to take Mehmet, so I told him I was a Police Officer and that his dad wanted to speak to him. I would never have hurt Mehmet but I was desperate.

"You know what Danny is capable of. Danny is being arrested in Mallorca for the murder of Chas Daly and kidnapping. I think it's about time you came clean with Mehmet about just what sort of man his father is. I'm sorry, if he hadn't put my son in danger, I would not have involved Mehmet. I think you two have got some talking to do and I want to see my son. I'll show myself out. If you want to report this to the local police..." started James, as he walked back out the front door. He looked back to Mehmet's mother who shook her head.

James got into his car and took a moment to let everything sink in. It had been an eventful day. In fact it had been quite a week. His new peaceful existence had been rocked by the events that he now wished to put behind him. He drove off heading back in the direction of Stansted Airport with the intention of getting on the first available flight back to Mallorca to see his family and give Adam the hug of his life. About twenty miles from the airport James' mobile phone rang. It was Bam Bam's number. He answered;

"Thank God that's over!" said James joyfully.

There was a slight pause, then Bam Bam said, "There was a problem. We didn't get him."

11

THE LONGEST DAY

The elation and relief that James had been feeling drained from him instantaneously. He pulled his car over and stopped due to the bombshell that he had just received.

"What do you mean you didn't get him?" he shouted in disbelief.

"Hear me out. We could see him in the car park of Festival Park. We had men on all four sides. We thought he was making his way back to the silver van that he had parked near one of the exits; the van he had Adam in. Armed Police in plain clothes were moving in to affect his arrest when he turned and headed into a crowd of people in the shopping centre. He was spooked and before we knew it he came out on a motorbike which he must have left earlier as a back up. The local units gave chase but he rode like a bat out of hell and went cross-country. The bottom line is that he got away. I'm sorry James, I was relying on Martinez and the local plod," said Bam Bam.

"I can't believe it! What now? I want a guard on my home. I don't think he would be stupid enough to try and harm them but he did threaten that if I involved the Police there would be consequences and he is a nutter. I wouldn't put it past him to try and exact some revenge for me doing that and for taking his son, even though he is now back with his mother, albeit a bit the wiser who and what his father really is," said James.

"I'll sort a guard out straight away with Martinez. Don't worry about that. Are you heading back here any time soon?"

"I'm on my way to the airport now and I know there is an early evening flight, which I hope to be on if there is any space. I don't care, I have to get back even if I have to fly from Scotland, wherever. I can't believe this. Just when I thought we could start to put this whole episode to bed," said James.

"Don't worry. We'll get him. He's been circulated as wanted all over the island. Martinez is really pissed off at his men. They are giving this top priority. It's just a matter of time before he re-surfaces. I'll let you know if I get any news. Drive safely. I want you back in one piece. See you soon Semtex," said Bam Bam.

He drove on to the airport and was able to get onto an early evening flight. James rang Charlotte who was relieved to have Adam back in one piece, but concerned by the news that Kusemi was still on the run. Martinez had placed an armed guard in plain clothes at his house who Charlotte had brought inside and who was happily drinking coffee.

His flight landed and James made his way back to his car in the airport car park and he drove quickly back to Fornalutx. He got in and found the police guard still inside. He went upstairs to the first floor living room where his family was.

"Come here," he motioned to Adam.

He bent down and hugged his son tightly, during which time his younger son came over and hugged his leg. Charlotte stood up and joined in.

"Family hug!" she shouted.

It felt good. James realised just what joy a family brings and just how important they were to him. He kissed all three and sat down on a sofa.

"What a day. I don't want too many more like that one. I'm sure you don't, Adam? Do you know where the man Kusemi took you to from school?" asked James.

"I think it was a house somewhere on its own. As I told the Police this afternoon I can't say any more than that because he put a blindfold on me and tied my hands behind my back."

"My wee man! Come here and give me another hug," said James and as Adam did so, Reuben not wishing to be left out, joined another hugging session.

"Listen, it's been a long day for us all. You boys should be in bed. It's nearly half ten. I'm not sure I want you going back to school until this man is caught, just in case. Now off to bed," said James giving the boys a kiss goodnight.

"Is the guard staying all night?" asked James.

"Yes. He was telling me he will be relieved at midnight when the night-shift officer will replace him. Inspector Martinez was here this afternoon to take a statement from Adam. He did offer to put us up in a hotel somewhere Kusemi wouldn't know, but I just wanted to stay here. James you don't think this guy will come back to try and harm us, do you?" asked Charlotte, suddenly breaking down.

"Hey, hey. Shhh. Don't worry," said James, trying to reassure his wife and hugging her once more.

"I'm not going to let anything happen to you or the boys, not on my watch. OK?"

"OK. I was so scared when you told me that he had taken Adam. I thought I would never see the wee man again," said Charlotte, sending herself into another bought of sobbing at the thought of this.

"They will get this bastard. By the way did Bam Bam call?" asked James trying to take her mind off her thoughts.

"Yes. He was here with Martinez. He stayed for a bit but he said he wanted to give us some space, so he is staying at C'an Reus if you need him. He said he will come up again in the morning."

"No problem. Right, come on let's go to bed and put this day behind us," said James, helping Charlotte up the stairs.

"What did you do exactly in London? You didn't scare his son, did you?" asked Charlotte.

"I went to his house and followed his mother as she dropped him off at Blackheath School. I couldn't live in London anymore. You forget about the traffic and the bloody drivers. Everyone cutting everybody up. No wonder there's so much 'road rage'. It would do your head in. I thought I was going to lose them at one point. It wasn't funny and we were so tight for time because I had to contact Kusemi by 10am Mallorcan time, so it was cutting it very fine. I told him I was Police and after Adam was safe I took him back home but I felt I had to explain my actions, so I had no choice but to tell him what his father had done. I don't think he had any idea what sort of a man he is. His mother who is separated from Kusemi lives alone with the boy and had kept him in the dark. Well he knows now, which I think is better for him in the long run," said James.

"I'm just going to nip downstairs and tell the policeman we are going to bed and just to check he knows what he's doing. Back in a mo."

James walked down to the entrada and greeted the policeman, who was sitting in relative darkness watching the front door.

"Hola. Que tal?" asked James.

"Moi bien senor," replied the officer.

"Do you speak English?" enquired James.

"A little," came the reply.

"OK. My wife and I are going to bed now and my boys are already in bed. I believe you are being relieved in about an hour?"

"Yes, that is correct."

"You know what this man looks like, don't you?"

"I have a photograph of the man here. My orders are to shoot him if I feel that my life or the lives of you or your family are in danger. I have a family too. You can count on me senor," said the officer.

"Thank-you. Good-night and help yourself to anything you like in the fridge."

"Thank-you senor but I'm fine."

With that, James climbed the stairs and to bed. He drifted off and was asleep as soon as his head hit the pillow.

He was woken from a deep sleep by Charlotte grabbing his arm and shaking it. As he came around, slightly disgruntled he said,

"What is it?"

"I heard a noise downstairs. It woke me and I've got my earplugs in," said Charlotte, sitting bolt upright in bed.

James looked at his bedside clock. It was just after midnight.

"It was probably the nightshift policeman arriving. I'll go and check just to be sure," said James, getting out of bed and walking to the next floor down, where he paused at the top of the stairs and called down in a low voice,

"Hola! Is everything alright?"

There was no response, so he began to get a little nervous. He went to the living room french doors, opened them and looked down at the street below in case the police officers were chatting outside about their changeover but there was no-one there. James went to his son's bedrooms and woke them both and told them to go upstairs to the second floor bedroom where their mother was. He then slowly walked down the last flight of stairs, one slow step at a time peering into the semi-darkness of his entrada. The front door was closed and the large antique internal wooden doors were closed from the inside, so someone must be there. James called out again,

"Hello! Hola! Is anyone there?"

There was still no reply. He continued down until he was only a few steps from the ground floor. The room was in darkness save for the light of the moon streaming a faint white light through the open shutters of his entrada window. There was no sign of the guard or his expected replacement.

The tiled floor was cold under his bare feet but he wanted to check if the front door was locked, as it would have been possible for the guard to pull the wooden internal doors closed from outside via a special opening section of the external glazed door made for exactly that purpose.

He bounded over towards the front door but as soon as he put his foot on the tiled floor of the entrada he slipped on the wet floor surface, landing on the small of his back in some pain. The floor was soaking wet.

As his eyes became slightly more accustomed to the dark and from its texture James realised that he had slipped in a pool of blood and could now see a trail of blood leading from the entrada into the utility room. James got to his feet just as a figure came towards him from out of the darkness from the direction of the utility room. It was Kusemi.

He lunged at James with a large knife. He managed to avoid the blow as Kusemi tried to stab him to the body with the knife. He then grabbed Kusemi's right arm in which he was holding a large kitchen-type knife. James couldn't take his eyes off it. He was in close now to Kusemi. He was struggling with him and could feel just how strong this man was but he knew he was fighting for his life and for the lives of his family. This man could not let go of the fact that Police had been at the drop-off. He had got away. He had got most of his money back but yet he still felt it necessary to try and exact revenge in his twisted mind, thought James.

James backed his body into Kusemi and drove him back against the wall keeping his right arm with the knife away from his naked torso. In a quick movement James threw Kusemi over his right shoulder in a pseudo-judo move. Kusemi landed on his back onto the hard floor, the knife still in his hand, and James' left hand still gripping Kusemi's right arm with all his strength. He jumped onto Kusemi's rib cage with his knees, with his full body weight and as he did so shouted in the direction of the stairs to alert Charlotte and his sons,

"Charlotte get out NOW! He's here!"

He leaned over Kusemi and head-butted him with as much force as he could muster, causing James to almost pass out. He hit his assailant with such force that this caused Kusemi to release his grip of the knife, which James flicked out of reach. He put both his hands round Kusemi's neck in a throttling grip. Kusemi was trying to throw James off him like a bucking bronco whilst attempting to release James' grip from his neck with one hand and with the other was punching him directly in the face and head. James brought his head in close to Kusemi's head to decrease the weight of the blows.

"You just couldn't let it lie," said James through gritted teeth.

"You killed me in the eyes of my son, so I've nothing left to live for," croaked Kusemi, like some alien being, his words were grossly distorted by James' efforts to choke him.

James realised then that the fact that he had pulled back the veil of deceit that Kusemi had managed to keep over his son and now that Memhet knew him for what he was, was the reason he wanted revenge or was willing to go out trying to get it. James pushed his thumb hard into a tender spot behind Kusemi's left ear, forcing him to turn his head to the right. He then manoeuvred his left arm and Kusemi rolled onto his side allowing James to put Kusemi's left arm in an arm lock up his back.

As he had been taught in Police training it was vital to control the man. Through his own experience James knew it was crucial to control the head. He was now in control and felt that all he had to do now was use his body weight and strength to subdue Kusemi until hopefully the cavalry, in the form of local Police arrived. Judging by the trail of blood leading to the utility room, his guard and probably the guard's relief were both not going to able to assist his plight.

After a few moments of James exerting significant force both to Kusemi's arm and on his neck, Kusemi stopped struggling as if to admit defeat. James took the opportunity to call out to make sure Charlotte had heard his earlier cries.

"Charlotte did you call the Police? I've got him now."

Just at that moment the front door opened, forcing back the internal wooden doors. James looked up to see a man standing at the open doorway pointing a gun at him. In that moment James thought he was going to be shot. Did Kusemi have back up after all? The man surely wasn't a Policeman, was he?

The man took a step forward into the entrada and said something to James in Spanish, to his absolute relief. Keeping his hands on Kusemi he motioned to the man with his head, whom he now realised was the night shift guard turning up late, that the man he wanted was under him.

"This man is Danny Kusemi. Have you got hand cuffs?" asked James.

" Si, si senor,comprendez," said the officer.

With that the officer holstered his firearm and placed Kusemi in handcuffs. James left Kusemi in the charge of the policeman and walked the few yards to the utility room. Turning on the light he could see the young guard from earlier lying on the floor. He knelt down beside him and checked for a pulse. It was faint and slow but he was still alive. James shouted to the officer that his colleague was still alive but that he needed an ambulance. He seemed to understand as he spoke quickly into his police radio asking for an ambulance and appeared to be telling his control room of what he had found.

"Stay with me," said James to the young policeman.

He was unconscious and his breathing was shallow. He had lost a lot of blood. It was hard to tell exactly where he had been stabbed as his shirt was completely soaked in blood. His breathing was now beginning to make a gurgling sound, as if he was breathing in blood. James ripped the shirt open to reveal a large gaping stab wound to the policeman's chest.

He ripped a piece of the shirt and placed it over the wound to try and put pressure on to it, in an effort to stem the relentless flow of blood. He checked his airway, then propped him sitting up against the door of the room in an effort to stop him from choking on his own blood and then into the recovery position. James was then joined by his neighbour, Brian.

"I heard the shouting and called the police. Can I help?" he asked.

"Keep pressure on this and talk to him," said James.

James walked back into the entrada. The other policeman looked anxiously at him.

"Miguel is OK?" he asked nervously of James.

"I hope so. He is still alive at the moment. He has been stabbed here," said James, pointing to his own chest. Have you called an ambulance?"

"Si. Si. I don't know," said the policeman shrugging and looking at his watch.

Kusemi was lying face down on the floor with his hands handcuffed behind him. The knife had now been placed on James' dining table. The policeman had one foot on Kusemi's back.

"You had better hope he lives," said James to Kusemi with disdain.

"Not that you give a fuck about anyone else. So what if your son knows what you are? Does this man deserve to die for that, so that you could try to kill my family and me? You're an animal! You don't deserve to live. That young policeman is married with a young family. He does deserve to live," said James, who could not contain his contempt for Kusemi. Kusemi lay on the floor silent.

"How is he doing Brian?" shouted James to his neighbour.

"Not great. Where's this ambulance?" asked Brian.

As if on cue, sirens were heard in the distance and after a few moments an ambulance crew followed in behind two local police officers. The ambulance crew went to tend to the injured policeman while the two uniformed officers assisted their plain clothed colleague in getting Kusemi up on his feet. Just then Inspector Martinez bounded through the door followed by Bam Bam, both men out of breath.

"Are you alright, James?" asked Bam Bam.

"Just about. Can someone please get this piece of shit out of my house," said James, motioning towards Kusemi.

Inspector Martinez spoke to his officers and the three officers removed Kusemi from the house. Martinez went to check on his injured officer, leaving James with his old friend.

"Are you cut? You've got a lot of blood on you," asked Bam Bam.

"I'm alright. I don't think it's mine. This could have turned out very differently. I feel very lucky to be alive," said James, shaking his head, "I have to go and check on Charlotte and the boys."

James walked upstairs to the top floor where he called out,

"Charlotte, are you there?"

The door to the roof terrace opened and Charlotte appeared.

"Oh my God, James are you alright?" she asked, looking at the blood on James's body.

"I'm OK. Are you OK? Are the boys there?"

"We're here," said Adam from behind his mother.

James walked into his bathroom and switched on the light and looked at his reflection in the mirror. He was taken aback by the state of his face and chest. He was covered in blood, from Kusemi and the policeman. He quickly showered trying to wash away the physical if not the mental evidence of the trauma he had just been through. He came out to find Charlotte waiting to offer a long hug and looked to him for reassurance that it was now safe to venture from her spot.

"The police have taken Kusemi away. He had stabbed the guard, who's in a bad way. Martinez is down there with Bam Bam and Brian came over to help. Take the boys back to bed. Boys come here," said James.

Adam followed by Reuben approached their father. James bent down and gave each a hug in turn.

"It's all over now. There's nothing to be frightened of anymore. The Police have arrested the bad man and taken him away. It's late and you both need your sleep. Off you go. I love you both," said James, as Charlotte walked the boys downstairs to their bedrooms.

James got dressed quickly and walked back down to the entrada. Inspector Martinez and Bam Bam were the only people left in the house.

"Where's Brian?" asked James.

"He's gone to bed and said he'll drop by in the morning," said Bam Bam.

"Is your man going to make it?" asked James.

"I hope so. He's a good man. I'm going to go to the hospital as soon as we are done here," said Inspector Martinez.

"I will need a statement from you and I will need to keep this as a crime scene until my forensic scene examiner has been, if that's OK. Are you up to doing this now?" he asked.

"I might as well. I don't think I'll be able to sleep after this," said James, taking a seat at his dining table.

"Hang on before we start. I think I need a drink. Anyone care to join me?" asked James, walking into his kitchen and reaching into a cupboard and producing a bottle of Old Bushmills whiskey.

"Please," replied both men.

James returned to the dining table with three tumblers with large measures of whiskey.

"This is how we were told to deal with stress in the old days and I think we all need this," said James handing out the tumblers.

All three men sat down at the table. Martinez produced a pen and paper and turned to James.

"First of all, I owe you an apology for not getting him at Festival Park. We thought we had all the exits covered. We should not have let him get away to put you and your family through this."

"Look, don't worry about it. It could have happened to anyone. I don't blame you or your men in the slightest. Kusemi is a nutter. He's the one to blame. Also I owe you an apology for not coming forward with more information about the locker key and the money in the bag. I don't know what I was thinking but it was a serious error of judgement on my part, so no-one is faultless," said James.

James provided a statement as to the events of that night, while a forensic officer arrived and took swabs and recovered the knife. The scene was photographed and mapped.

"What will happen from here?" asked James.

"I think we have enough evidence to charge him with one count of murder and two counts of attempted murder and kidnapping and that's only for starters," said Martinez.

"I don't think he is going to be released for a very long time, if ever. Here in Mallorca we take this sort of crime very seriously and a life sentence means a life sentence not like in Britain, eh?"

"Can I clean up this blood now? I don't want my family to see it in the morning?" asked James.

"Yes. Go ahead we have finished here now. I must go to the hospital now," said Martinez.

"Let me know about your officer. I hope he makes it."

"Thank you. Get some sleep," said Martinez stepping outside.

"Let me clean that floor for you," said Bam Bam.

"No. You get off to bed. I'm fine; I'd rather do it. I'll see you tomorrow," said James.

"OK partner but try and get some sleep. I'll look in on you late morning. Good-night."

James mopped up the blood from the floor and locked the front door. He climbed the stairs and went into his bedroom. Charlotte was lying in bed but still awake, waiting for him. James hugged and kissed her and held her without saying anything. He didn't have to. His actions spoke louder than any words. He fell asleep in her arms.

He woke late morning with a sore back, from his fall the night before. Charlotte was already up and James lay in bed reflecting on the events of the night before, reliving step by step what had happened.

He had been involved in dangerous events during his days in the Police. He had been shot at whilst chasing armed robbers in London, and he had received a commendation apprehending them. He had been in numerous dangerous situations in Northern Ireland including having to overcome violent offenders, been to countless violent murder scenes and been attacked with petrol bombs, but he had never had to fight for his life in his own home. The enormity of that fact suddenly hit him hard. What if Kusemi had overcome him? James knew that he would be dead and perhaps he would have taken his anger out on his family also. Suddenly his world of contentment in his 'Garden of Eden' had been severely rocked.

At that moment James questioned whether he could now stay in his house, in this village, on this island? His idyll had been tainted; spoiled. Could he ever feel the way he did before all this had happened? He doubted it. Time, as he had come to realise, was indeed a good healer but whether or not he could continue living there was something that he would have to face up to. James had tried to escape from clearing up the mess of those responsible for doing evil acts. He had tried to protect his sons without cocooning them completely.

He realised more than most that there are good and bad people in the world and no matter where you go, you cannot escape man's inhumanity to his fellow man, but he also realised that there are people who are kind, selfless and loving. You cannot have good without evil, nor beauty without ugliness, nor compassion without cruelty, for how can you appreciate one without the other.

James instantly resolved that the reasons for him moving his family to Fornalutx had not changed, despite what had happened. It would be up to him to continue with his dreams, his ambitions. Why should he let someone like Kusemi ruin his family's happiness by moving again? No, thought James, I won't let that happen.

He threw back the bed sheet and gingerly got out of bed, still aching from his fight with Kusemi. He looked through the window that overlooked the roof terrace, where his family were breakfasting and took a moment to enjoy the sight, before joining them.

The sky was a cloudless azure, with only the trail of a jet aircraft impacting on the otherwise perfect canvas. There was the sound of swifts and swallows calling from a neighbouring roof and the chimes of the church clock marking half past the hour. It was as if nothing had happened. The world was still turning and the beauty of the place was undiminished. James' spirits lifted.

His family needed him to be strong. They had been in danger, perhaps more danger than they would ever realise. It was time to put the events of the previous days behind him. It was his duty to get them back to something close to normality as soon as possible. He did feel a sense of responsibility for having brought upon his family some of the anguish caused by him being tempted by greed. It made him realise that the most important things in life cannot be bought. What was required today was that he spent time with his family.

A day at the beach was called for and some fun and to meet up with some of the network of fantastic people who he was lucky enough to call friends. Life was for living and life in Mallorca was something to be revered.

After breakfast, armed with buckets and spades, body-board, beach towels, sun-cream and other essentials for a day at the beach, James set off with his family in tow to his car. Once ensconced in the car he drove along the winding 'American Road', leading from Fornalutx through the majestic Tramuntana Mountains, providing photogenic glimpses of Soller and the valley below, emerging between Soller and its Port and then down to Repic beach at Port de Soller.

It was another perfect Mallorcan summer's day. It was already showing 30 degrees Celsius on the temperature gauge. It was going to be a hot one. There wasn't a cirrus or cumulus cloud in the sky and as they approached the coast there was a soothing off-shore breeze, providing some respite from the intensity of the full heat of the sun and giving some waves which would be a bonus to Adam on his body-board.

The family paid the stoic sunbed attendant and unravelled their beach towels on their sunbeds, anxious to get straight into the water to cool down and to engage in some family revelry. After applying copious amounts of high factor sun-cream, James and his two sons bounded towards the sea and James ran headlong into the water and dived under it, surfacing to see his son's more tentative approach in entering the water. He walked back towards them, encouraging them to follow suit in a similar manner but he was met with less than an enthusiastic response.

"Come on! Dive in, the water's lovely," said James, wiping the salty water from his eyes.

"It's cold Dad," replied Adam.

Reuben, resplendent in his orange armbands, screamed with excitement in anticipation of getting further into the sea from his ankle-deep position.

"Am I going to have to come over there and drag you in?" said James in a playful way.

"No Daddy! Don't come any closer!" shouted Reuben, clearly distressed at the thought of being forced further into the cold water.

James laughed and stood back allowing the boys the time to get used to the water and gradually Adam took the plunge and went under the water, resurfacing with his eyes closed and jumping up and down. Having mastered the water himself, he turned his energy in encouraging his younger brother to do the same.

"It's not as cold as you think, Reuben. Go on, just start swimming," said Adam.

With a little further encouragement Reuben too became immersed in the salty brine and before long father and sons were swimming and paddling and splashing.

After half an hour or so, all three somewhat tired from their exertion, scrambled back over the hot sand, as if walking on hot coals, only stopping once they had reached the cooler sand underfoot that was shaded by the umbrella. James lay down on his back on his

sun-lounger, scanning everything in his view. In his fore-
ground and close to him was everything that was most
dear to him, his seemingly contented family. In the near
distance were the Port de Soller and the Marina with its
pleasure craft entering and leaving the perfect little bay.
Behind him were the mountains and all around him
were people enjoying life. It was busy without being
saturated and over-crowded. People were walking along
the wide pedestrianised promenade. Some children,
who were still on holiday, were eating ice cream and
riding tricycles from the bike hire shop. Other people
were just relaxing over their lunch along the promenade
outside many of the restaurants that lined it. James felt
relaxed. The events of the last few days seemed like a
long distant memory, a memory that he would not be
able to put away into his very full filing cabinet in his
brain, until after the inevitable trial. However with any
luck and if Kusemi knew what was good for him, he
would plead guilty to the charges and therefore James
would not be required to attend Court. Right at that
moment he felt very lucky indeed and he counted his
blessings. As two of his favourite films aptly caught his
mood in their titles, James on reflection agreed with
Roberto Bellini and Frank Capra that *'Life is Beautiful'*
and *'It's A Wonderful Life.'*

12

KEEP YOUR ENEMIES CLOSER

Kusemi was awakened by a stream of bright sunlight filtering through the bars of his cell at Soller Police station. He had spent a restless night and had seemingly kept an almost all-night vigil, in part thanks to the hourly chiming of the church clock several streets away and partly due to him taking stock of his situation. In particular, he had been analysing the fact that his son Mehmet knew him for what he was and it was this fact above all others that disturbed Kusemi.

His solitude was disturbed sometime later by the opening of the hatch in his cell door and a plastic tray being placed on it with the contents of his breakfast. He had no appetite but shuffled over the few feet to the hatch and accepted the tray containing a few meagre offerings but was only interested in the lukewarm coffee.

He sat on the edge of his bunk in a state of desolation. He had lived a charmed life. He had always managed to come out on top: until now. Kusemi knew in his heart that this time he had been caught 'banged to rights.' In the past he had been able to manipulate both people and the system but it was different this time. He was going to be charged with the murder of Chas Daly. He had been remorseful when he had heard that Daly had not made it. He had left him in a bad way but he thought he had only given a good beating. In the end he couldn't quite bring himself to finish him off. He was missing him in such a situation as he found himself in.

He would be charged with the kidnapping of James Gordon's son and he would be charged with the attempted murder or murder of the Policeman, depending on whether or not he survived and the attempted murder of James Gordon. So, all in all, his situation was pretty bleak, he thought, as he drained the last mouthful of strong, black coffee.

An hour later, after Kusemi had washed, a police custody officer opened the cell door and directed him to a room further up the corridor. He opened the door and showed him in, where a man in beige trousers and a white shirt stood up and greeted him in English;

"Good morning Mr. Kusemi. My name is Timothy Entwhistle, I am an interpreter and I have been requested to interpret your rights and the proceedings here this morning. The officer here is obliged to go over the reasons for your arrest, caution you and allow you access to legal advice and I am here to make sure you understand your rights. Is that clear?" asked the Interpreter.

"Yeah, I understand," said Kusemi, taking a seat at the table.

After he had been given all the information as to his arrest, he elected not to be provided with a solicitor, despite the protests of both the police officer and his interpreter, he firmly refused legal counsel.

He was placed back in his cell for a further period only to be brought out and taken then to an interview room. His uniformed guard showed him into the room, where already seated was the officer who had arrested him earlier and the familiar face of a gloating Detective Sergeant Wiggins of Rotherhithe C.I.D.

"Sit down," said Inspector Martinez.

Kusemi sat down opposite both men, his eyes fixed on DS Wiggins, who sat with arms folded, staring at him with the hint of a smirk and an 'I told you we'd get you' look on his face.

Martinez, who had been shuffling through reams of paper on the table, looked up and said;

"I am Inspector Ramon Martinez of La Policia Nacional based in Palma, Mallorca. Also present in the interview is Detective Sergeant Wiggins from The Metropolitan Police in London. You were arrested in Fornalutx at 00:25 hours this morning in a house in Carrer de San Sebastia for the attempted murder of a policeman and of a James Gordon. I am now further arresting you for the murder of a Charles Daly, ten days ago at this address in Fornalutx and also for the kidnap of Adam Gordon two days ago. I must tell you that you are entitled to legal advice and that what you say will be given as evidence in any subsequent trial. Do you wish to say anything at this stage?"

"No comment," said Kusemi.

This made DS Wiggins turn to his counterpart and say,

"I told you it would be a 'no comment interview' Ramon. Look Danny, you and I have no great love for one another. I have been after you for years and you have finally screwed up big time. I am here because I know you and so you can't try and bullshit on this one. Inspector Martinez here speaks excellent English, so you don't need an interpreter but why do you not want to have a solicitor present during this interview?"

"No comment," replied Kusemi.

"Listen. It's your choice and we will continue without one but if you think a 'no comment interview' will save you or that you can claim you weren't allowed the correct legal advice or you didn't understand what was happening; that won't wash here Danny. The Spanish don't fuck about. I'd be speaking to a lawyer, if I was you," said DS Wiggins.

"No comment," repeated Kusemi.

Kusemi had been through many police interviews in his time and had always adopted the policy of a 'no comment' interview, with the view that he would never assist the police in any inquiry apart from perhaps answering his name, and he would never 'grass' on anyone else. Even though he was a paid Police Informant, he had never actually given up any information on anyone and used this to his advantage by bribing his handler for information which, up until now, helped him stay one step ahead of the game.

"OK. State your full name?" asked Martinez.

"Daniel Mustafa Kusemi," he replied.

"Is this your date of birth and home address?"

"Yeah," replied Kusemi, looking at the custody record.

"OK. Let's start with ten days ago. Can you tell me where you were on that Friday night say between nine o'clock and two in the morning?" said Martinez.

"No comment."

"Were you in Fornalutx and in the house owned by Charles Daly?"

"No comment."

"Do you know Charles or Chas Daly?"

"No comment."

"Is it not true that this man stole a substantial amount of money from you? This money, my colleague here tells me, is believed to be from criminal activities back in the UK. We know that this man stole from you and came to hide out in that village. We know that you came to the island and hired a car on this date, in your own name."

Martinez pulled out a sealed bag from under some paperwork on the table.

"I have here a copy of your car hire agreement and a copy of your driving licence. Did you hire this car on this date?"

"No comment."

"Let's get to the night in question. I believe you drove to the village in the hire-car and that you telephoned Daly on arrival. We know that he received a call on his mobile at about 11pm. I believe you rang him and he returned home where you beat him viciously about the head and body for some considerable time," said Martinez.

"No comment," interjected Kusemi.

"After which you took a cushion and held it over the now defenceless Daly and suffocated him. The Pathologist's report shows numerous blows to his head, face and body, including three fractured ribs and a fractured cheekbone, but the cause of death was asphyxiation. He had been suffocated. Tell us why you did it?"

Kusemi, who had been nonchalantly repeating his 'no comment' response without thinking, sat silent with a fixed gaze on Martinez. He had just heard him say that the cause of death was that Daly had been suffocated not that he had died from the injuries that he had inflicted on him, nor even that he had choked on his own blood as Kusemi had thought may have been the case.

This meant that Kusemi hadn't killed him. He couldn't understand. When he left Daly he was in a bad way but he was unconscious but he was still alive. He had not suffocated him. Either the police were lying and Daly was not dead or someone else had murdered his once best mate and he was going to take the rap for something, for once he didn't do. How fuckin' ironic, thought Kusemi.

"Do you recognise this man?" asked Martinez, who showed Kusemi a photograph of the corpse of Chas Daly.

That left the only option that someone else killed him, he thought, as he returned to type and repeated,

"No comment."

"Did you murder Chas Daly?" asked Martinez.

Kusemi looked at his old adversary DS Wiggins, who was watching his every move and he stared into his eyes and firmly said,

"No fucking comment."

DS Wiggins looked puzzled and looked at Martinez. The interview continued for another period but now Kusemi was not really listening. He was focusing on the revelation that he was not responsible for Daly's death, which although he was glad not to be, he knew that he would be charged with his murder. Perhaps he could try to save his neck on this one but who would believe him and he wasn't going to start coughing up now just to try to save himself.

What sort of life would he have without the love of the only person for whom he cared: his son Mehmet? He had already contemplated suicide but he had been stripped of anything that might assist him in this and anyway he had quickly dismissed this as a coward's option. No, he would simply do his time. It would be hard time but no one would break him.

The interview continued with several breaks, going over the other charges relating to the attempted murders of the police officer and James Gordon the previous night and of the kidnapping of James Gordon's son, Adam from his school. He knew he was caught 'banged to rights' for these but continued in his 'no comment' approach.

Who was responsible for Chas' murder he wondered? It must be the ex-Detective, James Gordon, he surmised. Who else had the knowledge of the locker key and the money and the opportunity to finish Chas off the night he had dished out the beating to him? He was the only one who had had access to the money and he had taken Kusemi for a fool and screwed him.

When Kusemi had gone to the hand-over at Festival Park and learned that James had taken his son Mehmet in London, he had been caught off-guard. When he had opened the brown hold-all containing the money, he had quickly scanned its contents and had believed it contained the vast majority of his stolen £1 million minus what Chas paid for the house in Fornalutx and what he would have spent in the weeks leading up to his murder.

It was only after Kusemi managed to escape from the Police who were there to arrest him and got back to his hideout that he realised he had been cheated. The bag did contain some money on the top few layers of the bag but underneath there was cut up old newspaper. The bag only contained about £100,000. It was short by about £650,000 by his calculations. Kusemi had no doubt that James Gordon was responsible for Chas' murder and for stealing the remainder of his money.

Perhaps he and Bam Bam were in this together. This was summary justice, dished out Metropolitan Police style, for all the crimes both he and Chas had committed but there had never been enough evidence to have them charged, thought Kusemi. He began to have an admiring, albeit begrudging respect for the way in which he had been 'stitched up like a kipper.'

The interviews finally ended and Bam Bam approached Kusemi who was getting ready to be charged with the offences.

"Danny, off the record, you seemed to be upset by the revelation that Chas had been suffocated. Did you actually kill him?"

"Would it make any difference to the outcome? I don't fuckin' think so. It doesn't matter if I did or I didn't. I'm gonna do the time for it."

With that, Bam Bam made his way from Soller Police station, leaving Kusemi to be charged with murder, two counts of attempted murder and kidnapping. He would appear at Court in the morning and from there go to Palma prison whilst awaiting his trial.

Bam Bam drove back to his hotel in Fornalutx and packed his bag ready for his flight back to London later that day. Kusemi's comments had put an element of doubt in his mind. The police had not recovered the money from him but he assumed that it had been all there at the hand-over because Kusemi had released Adam.

He had refused to answer questions relating to this during the interview but Wiggins had the distinct feeling that Kusemi had been genuinely surprised during the interview to find out that Chas' cause of death had been suffocation. Could his old friend James be involved in something unsavoury? No, he knew him too well and he was too moral for anything of that nature or was he?

He decided to call at James' house before leaving and he found him in but Charlotte and his sons were out.

"Come in, come in!" said James as he greeted him at the door. "Well how did it go?"

"Fine. It was just as I suspected: no comment all the way. Except one thing he said, I can't quite fathom. He appeared to be genuinely surprised that Chas had been suffocated. It was just the way he reacted and he looked directly at me when he was asked did he kill him and he said, 'no fucking comment' in a very deliberate manner. I don't know why he would have done that. The other thing is about the money. As you know we haven't been able to recover that.

There was no sign of it at the rented house he had been staying in and he's not telling us where it is. But I got the impression that he's not happy about that either. He won't say anything but I felt that he thought we were screwing him on this; that perhaps the money or at least all the money wasn't there at the hand-over. You did hand it all over didn't you?"

"Of course I did!" exclaimed James, reeling from the accusation from his old friend. "Look, I'll be honest the thought of all that money did tempt me for a moment but it was only for a moment. Charlotte soon beat that out of me. Come on Bam Bam, you know me better than that!"

"I know, I'm sorry but I had to ask. Listen it's probably me reading things that aren't even there. I'd better make a move; I've got to catch my flight. You take care Semtex."

Bam Bam gave James a hug and a pat on the back.

"Listen my old mucker, give my best to Charlotte and the boys and I'm glad to have seen you again, despite the circumstances. Look after yourself."

"You too, take care. Have a good flight and we'll speak soon. Adios."

James returned to the kitchen, where he was preparing the evening meal. He felt slightly hurt by the fact that his old friend had felt that he could have been responsible for taking the money after all or at least part of it. It was not the fact that he had momentarily doubted his honesty that hurt James but the fact that he thought he could have done this at the very time his son Adam's life was in danger. James tried to put it down to Kusemi simply trying to put doubts into the investigators' minds in what was essentially an open and shut case.

After the evening meal James and Charlotte went for an evening stroll, leaving the two boys playing with friends in the plaça, supervised by Garth and Jenny, returning a short time later to enjoy a coffee in the square before bed.

James tucked his two sons up in bed and made his own way to bed on the top floor, where Charlotte was already in bed, reading.

She looked up after a few moments;

"Is everything alright? You were very quiet this evening," she asked.

"Yeah, I'm fine. It's just something that Bam Bam said before he left that got me thinking. I'm sorry, it's nothing really," said James, getting into bed.

"OK, I'll see you in the morning," said Charlotte, turning off the light.

"Night," said James, kissing her goodnight, before moving onto his side, deep in thought.

James was tired and quickly drifted off to sleep. He began to dream and his dream was about what was bothering him. In his dream he was back in the plaça in Fornalutx on the night when Daly was murdered. He could see Daly going back home and meeting Kusemi. He could see the beating he received from Kusemi but then Kusemi left. Daly was still breathing. Kusemi went off in search of James and the locker key but in the shadows a figure of a man emerged, who had stopped to relieve himself. Kusemi did not see him but the man saw him leave the house, the door of which he left ajar. The man then went to the door and saw Daly lying in the room beyond his entrada, barely conscious.

He went in and appeared concerned for Daly's well-being and was about to call for an ambulance but Daly whispered to him about the key and about the money and James can see how the figure, whose face he cannot see, reaches over and lifts a cushion and places it over Daly's nose and mouth, who by now is too weak to struggle. This man suffocates Daly and then turns off the light and closes the door and exit's the house.

By this time in the dream James can see Kusemi asking Pepe if he has seen James and where he lives but James is by now in bed.

He can see the figure leaving Daly's house and making his way to James' house and entering it by accessing the rear and climbing onto the roof terrace. In his dream-like state James can see the figure try to find the cigarette packet containing the locker key which is on his bedside locker but the intruder makes a noise, wakening James who gets up and finding the roof terrace door unlocked, locks it and goes back to sleep. James sees the figure leave empty-handed.

His dream switches to the day he took his family to The Castell d'Alaro with Matt's family and to something Matt said, when James showed him the key and told him about finding the body. Matt hadn't seemed that shocked and thinking back James had remembered Matt's offer to take the key and assist in trying to discover its origin but James had refused, to the annoyance of Matt.

James could now see Kusemi making his way on the motorbike back to his hideout after getting away from the Police at Festival Park. From his bird's eye view in his dream he can see Kusemi remove the contents of the brown leather holdall which now contained old newspaper and only £100,000 of the £735,000 that James knew there should have been. Suddenly James could hear Matt's answer when he asked him about how his business was doing in the recession.

"Oh you know, not great but something will turn up." James can now see the missing money in a plastic bag. In his dream-like state he can see it through walls. It is in a hiding place in the floor of a built-in wardrobe, in a house he has seen before. He can see the figure from before. The figure opens the wardrobe door and reaches in and lifts up several floor tiles and pulls out the money in a plastic bag. Light now emanates from behind the figure for the first time and gets stronger, lighting up the full face of a smiling man.

James sits bolt upright in bed in a cold sweat with his eyes wide open.

"Matt?" he exclaims.